W9-CJX-663

# PATTY FAIRFIELD

# BOOKS BY CAROLYN WELLS

## PATTY SERIES

Patty Fairfield

Patty at Home

Patty in the City

Patty's Summer Days

Patty in Paris

Patty's Friends

Patty's Pleasure Trip

Patty's Success

Patty and Azalea

Patty's Motor Car

Patty's Butterfly Days

Patty's Social Season

Patty's Suitors

Patty's Romance

Patty's Fortune

Patty Blossom

Patty-Bride

## MARJORIE SERIES

Marjorie's Vacation

Marjorie's Busy Days

Marjorie's New Friend

Marjorie in Command

Marjorie's Maytime

Marjorie at Seacote

## TWO LITTLE WOMEN SERIES

Two Little Women

Two Little Women and Treasure House

Two Little Women on a Holiday

# Patty Fairfield

*By* CAROLYN WELLS

Author of *Idle Idylls*

NEW YORK

DODD, MEAD & COMPANY

1929

To My Little Friend

MARION AMES TAGGART

# Contents

# Patty Fairfield

---

## CHAPTER I

### HER FATHER'S PLAN

" How old are you, Patty?" asked ner father, abruptly.

" Fourteen, papa,—why?"

" My conscience! what a great girl you're getting to be. Stand up and let me look at you."

Patty Fairfield, with two twists and a spring, brought herself to her feet, and stood awaiting her father's inspection.

He saw a slender, graceful girl, a Southern blonde of the purest type. Her pretty golden hair would gladly have hung in curly masses, but it was only allowed to have its own sweet will around her temples and at the end of a long thick braid.

1

Her eyes were blue, deep and twinkly, and the rest of her face was as pretty and sweet as soft girlish contours and a perfect complexion could make it.

But best of all was the gentle expression and frank, good-natured smile which so often broke into mischievous dimples.

It did on this occasion, and Patty laughed merrily at her father's grave consideration of her.

"What is it, papa?" she asked. "Did you think I was still an infant, and were you going to buy me a new dolls' house? Or were you going to take me to the circus? I'm not a bit too old for the circus."

"Aren't you? Then I will take you, but what is on my mind at present is a much more serious matter. Sit down again, Puss, and I'll tell you all about it.

"You know for years I've looked forward to the time when you should grow up to be old enough to keep house for me. And I thought then we'd go back North and settle down among my people and your mother's relatives. I haven't been North since your mother died,

but now I want to go, and I want you to spend
the rest of your life there. In many ways it will
be better for you than Virginia. You will have
more advantages; your life will be broader and
more varied. Now I can't be ready to leave
here for good in less than a year; I want to sell
out my lumber interests and settle up my business affairs.

" But I am continually receiving letters from
your aunts,—you have lots of aunts, Patty,—and
they are apparently all anxious that you shall
visit them. So, if you consent, this is my plan.
You've never traveled any, have you, Puss ? "

" Never been out of Virginia in my life,
papa."

" No ? Well, you ought to see a little of how
the rest of the world lives and moves. So I
think I'll let you visit in the North for a year,—
say three months with each of your four aunts,
—and then next fall I'll be ready to join you,
and we'll buy a house and you shall be mistress
of it."

" A home of our own ? Oh, papa, I'd like
hat lots ! "

" Yes, so would I. As we have always lived

in boarding-houses since your mother's death,
you've had no opportunity to learn the details
of housekeeping, and these four visits will show
you four very distinct types of families."

"Why, are my aunts all so different, papa?"

"Indeed they are, and though I hope you can
make yourself happy with each one, yet you
will find life very different in the various homes."

"Tell me about them, papa," said Patty, con-
tentedly settling herself back among the cushions
of the couch, for she dearly loved a long talk
with her father.

"Well, you will go first to the St. Clairs.
You remember Uncle Robert, your mother's
brother, who was here four or five years ago,
don't you?"

"Indeed I do; he brought me a French doll
nearly as big as I was then myself,—and a whole
five-pound box of candy. He is a lovely man.
But I've never seen Aunt Isabel or the children,
—only their photographs."

"Your Aunt Isabel is,—but no,—I won't tell
you anything about your relatives. You may
discover their faults and virtues for yourself.
Most of all, my child, you will need to cultivate

your sense of proportion.  Do you know what
proportion means ? "

"Oh, yes, papa, I studied 'ratio and proportion' in arithmetic."

"Not that kind," said her father, smiling; "I
mean a proportion of human interests, of amusements or occupations.  I wonder if you *are* too
young to understand."

"No, I'm not too young to understand *anything*," said Patty, fairly blinking in her endeavor
to look as wise as an owl.

"Well, then, listen while I put it this way.
Suppose you were to make a cake, an ordinary
sized cake, you know, how much yeast would
you put in it ? "

"Not any, papa," said Patty, laughing merrily.  "I know enough housekeeping not to put
yeast in a cake.  I'd use baking-powder."

"Yes," said her father, quite undisturbed,
"that is what I meant,—baking-powder.  Now
how much of it would you use ? "

"Well, about two teaspoonfuls," said Patty,
feeling very important and housewifely.

"Yes.  Now suppose instead of two teaspoonfuls you put in two cupfuls."

"Why then I wouldn't have any cake at all! I reckon it would rise right up the chimney and run down on the roof outside."

"Well, that shows just what I mean.  There'd be a too great proportion of baking-powder, wouldn't there?"

"Indeed there would," assented Patty, much interested in the conversation, but a little bewildered.

"To try again," her father continued, "suppose your frock was so covered by trimming that the material could scarcely be seen at all."

"Then," said Patty, who was rapidly learning her lesson, "then there'd be too great a proportion of trimming for the frock."

"Ah," said her father, "you begin to see my drift, do you?  And if you had all tables in your house, and no chairs or bedsteads or bureaus, there'd be too great a proportion of tables, wouldn't there?"

"Yes; and I perceive," said Patty, slowly and with mock gravity, "that proportion means to have too many of one thing, when you'd better have a lot of others."

"No, you're all wrong!  That is a lack of

proportion. Proportion is to have exactly **the** right amount of each ingredient."

" Yes,—and what has all this to do with Aunt Isabel? Does she put too much baking-powder in her cake, or has she nothing but tables in her house?"

" Those, my dear, were only figures of speech. But if you're going to make a home for your old father next year, I want you to learn from observation what are the principal ingredients to put into it, and then learn to adjust the proportions."

" Papa, I believe I do know what you mean, but it's all out of proportion when you call yourself 'my old father,' for you're not old a bit. You're a beautiful young man, and I'm sure any one who didn't know us would take you for **my** brother."

" Come, come, Puss, you mustn't be so flattering, or I'll keep you here, and not let you go North at all; and I do believe you're just dying to go."

" I'd like it lots if you were going too. But to be away from you a whole year is no fun at all. Can't I wait until next fall and we'll go together?"

" No, Patsie; your aunts are urging me to let you visit them and I think the experiences will do you good. And beside, my plans for the next year are very uncertain. I may have to go to Bermuda to see about my plantation there,— and all things considered, I think you would be better off in the North. I shall miss you, of course, but a year soon slips away, you know, and it will fly very quickly for you, as you will be highly entertained with your new experiences."

Now, Patty Fairfield was a philosophic little girl, so when she found that her father's mind was made up she accepted the situation and offered no objections of any kind. And, indeed the new plan was not without its charm. Although she knew none of her aunts, she knew a great deal about them, and their Northern homes seemed attractive to her in many ways.

" What about school, papa? " she said, finally.

" That will be left to the judgment of each aunt in turn. I think Aunt Isabel has a governess for her children, and Aunt Hester will probably teach you herself. But you will learn enough, and if not, you can consider it a year's vacation, and I'll put you back in school when I am with you again."

"Well," said Patty, meditatively, "I think it will be very nice, and I'll like it, but I'll be awful lonesome for you," and with a spring she jumped into her father's arms.

"Yes, of course, my baby, we'll be homesick for each other, but we'll be brave, and when we feel *very* lonesome, we'll sit down and write each other nice long letters."

"Oh, that will be fun, I love letters ; and here comes Clara, may I tell her about it ? "

"Yes, and tell her she must come to see me once in a while, and cheer me after I lose my own little girl."

Clara Hayden was Patty's intimate friend and both the girls' hearts grew sad at the thought of parting.

"But," said Patty, who was determined to look on the bright side, " after a year, papa and I will have a house of our own, and then you can come and make us a long, long visit. And we can write letters, Clara, and you must tell me all about the girls, and about school and about the Magnolia Club."

" Yes, I will ; and you write to me about all you do at your aunts' houses. Where do they live, Patty ? "

" Well, I shall go first to Aunt Isabel's, and she lives in Elmbridge. That's in New Jersey, but it's quite near New York. Next I'm going to Aunt Hester's ; she lives in Boston. Then I'm going to visit Aunt Grace. They live in Philadelphia, but I'll be with them in the summertime, and then they're at their country place somewhere on Long Island, wherever that may be. And the last one is Aunt Alice, and I forget the name of the town where she lives. Isn't it nice, Clara, to have so many aunts ? "

" Yes, lovely ! I suppose you'll go to New York often."

" I don't know; I think I'm afraid of New York. They say it's an awful dangerous place."

" Yes, it is. People get killed there all the time."

" Fiddlesticks ! I don't believe they do. Well, I reckon I won't get killed. Uncle Robert will take better care of me than that."

# CHAPTER II

## TRAVELING NORTH

As a result of many letters back and forth between Mr. Fairfield and the Northern aunts, Patty stood one morning on the platform of the railway station, all ready to depart for her new homes.

It was the first week in December, and the little girl shivered as she thought of the arctic cold to which she imagined herself going.

" Of course they'll meet me in a sleigh, won't they, papa? " she said.

" Perhaps so, but I doubt it," he replied. " They don't have such snowstorms in Jersey now as they used to when I was a boy. Last winter they had no sleighing at all. But here comes Miss Powers; let us go to greet her." Miss Powers was a sharp-faced lady who came marching along the platform with a firm step.

Patty was to travel in her care, not because she was an especially desirable traveling companion, but because she was the only acquaintance of the Fairfields who chanced to be going North at that time.

"Good-morning," she cried, "are you here already? I was certain you'd be late and miss the train. Not a very pleasant day, is it? I wish we had planned to go to-morrow instead. Why, Patty, you are wearing your best hat! You'll spoil it, I'm sure. Have you your trunk check? Give it to me, you'll certainly lose it else."

"Here it is, Miss Powers," said Mr. Fairfield, pleasantly, "and I dare say you will prove more responsible than my rattle-pated daughter."

He squeezed Patty's hand affectionately as he said this, and a great wave of homesickness came over the child's heart. She caught her father round the neck, and vainly trying to keep the tears back, she whispered,

"Oh, papa, dear, let me stay with you. I don't want to go to Aunt Isabel's,—I know she's horrid, and I just want you, you, *you!*"

Miss Powers was shocked at this exhibition of emotion, and said with asperity:

"Come, come, it's too late to talk like that

now. And a big girl like you ought to be ashamed to act so babyish."

But Mr. Fairfield kissed Patty tenderly and said: " Dear, we're going to be very brave, you know,—and besides, you're only going for a visit. All people go visiting at some time in their lives, and next December I'll be shaking the dust of Richmond off of my feet and coming after you, pell-mell." Patty smiled through her tears, and then the train came tooting along and they all climbed aboard.

As the train waited for ten minutes, Mr. Fairfield had ample time to find the seats engaged for the travelers, and to arrange their hand-luggage in the racks provided for it. Then he bade Miss Powers good-bye, and, turning to Patty, clasped her in his arms as he said:

" Pattykins, good-bye. The year will soon pass away, and then we'll have a jolly little home together. Be brave and gentle always, and as a parting gift I give you this little box which contains a talisman to help you bear any troubles or difficulties that may come to you."

As he spoke, he put into Patty's hand a small parcel sealed at each end with red sealing-wax.

" Don't open it now," he continued. " Keep
it just as it is until you reach Aunt Isabel's.
Then after you have gone to your room on the
first night of your stay with her, open the box
and see what is in it."

Then the warning whistle blew, and with a
final embrace of his little daughter, Mr. Fairfield
left the car.

The train started, and for a moment Patty saw
her father waving his handkerchief, and then he
was lost to her sight.   She felt just like indulg-
ing in a good cry, but Miss Powers would have
none of that.

The worthy spinster was already opening her
bag and preparing to make herself comfortable
for her journey.

" Now, Patty," she said, but not unkindly,
" you've left your pa behind, and you're going
away from him to stay a year.   You've got to
go, you can't help yourself, so you might just as
well make the best of it, and be cheerful instead
of miserable.   So now that's settled, and you'd
better get out your books and games or whatever you brought along to amuse yourself with."

Miss Powers had taken off her hat and gloves

and arranged a small balsam pillow behind her head. She put on her glasses, and opened a book in which she at once became absorbed.

Patty, being thus left to her own devices, became much interested in the novelty of her surroundings. It was great fun to lean back against the high-cushioned seat and look out of the window at the trees and plantations and towns as they flew by. This kept her amused until noontime, when a waiter came through the car banging a gong.

Miss Powers shut her book with a snap, and announced that they would go to the dining-car for their lunch.

This was even more fun, for it seemed so queer to Patty to sit at a table and eat, while at the same time she was flying through the country at such break-neck speed.

" It's like the enchanted carpet, isn't it, Miss Powers ? " she said, as they slid through a thick grove and then out into the sunshine again.

" What is? what carpet ? " asked Miss Powers, looking down at the floor of the car.

" Oh, not a real carpet," said Patty, politely repressing a smile at the elder lady's ignorance of fairy-lore. " I mean, for us to go scooting along so fast is like the travelers on the magicians' carpet. Don't you know, the carpet would move of itself wherever he told it to."

" H'm," commented Miss Powers, " that would be a good kind of a carpet to have at house-cleaning time, wouldn't it ? "

This prosaic disposition of the magic carpet quite shocked Patty, but she adapted herself to the idea, and said, " Yes, indeed ; you could just say, ' Carpet, get up and go out and hang yourself on the clothes-line, and then shake yourself well and come back again,'—oh, that would be convenient."

Miss Powers smiled in an absent-minded sort of way, and Patty chattered on, half to herself and half to her companion.

" But suppose the carpet should be naughty and refuse to go,—that wouldn't be so pleasant."

" Or suppose it should run away and never come back ? "

This latter remark was made by a strange voice, and Patty looked up quickly to see the man who was seated opposite, smiling in a very friendly way.

He was an elderly gentleman with white hair and beard, and it seemed to Patty's vivid imagination that he looked like Noah, or some other of the ancient patriarchs.

"That would be a great joke on the housekeeper," Patty answered, feeling already well acquainted with the pleasant old gentleman, "and I suppose she would have to get a new carpet."

"Or have a hard-wood floor laid in her room," he responded.

"Or live on a bare floor," said Miss Powers. "I think it would be a very slack housekeeper who would let her carpets shake themselves, and she would probably be too lazy or too poor to replace the ones that ran away."

Mr. Noah, as Patty called the old man in her mind, laughed heartily at this, and during the rest of the luncheon hour proved himself a genial and entertaining companion.

The day passed quickly, and at bedtime Patty was quite tired enough to welcome the thought of tucking herself away in one of those queer-looking bunks that the porter was arranging.

"I'll sleep on the top shelf," she said, gleefully, "may I, Miss Powers?"

"I'll be very glad if you will, child,—I've **no** desire to climb up there. Ugh, I don't think I can sleep anywhere on this bobbety-bobble train."

Then the porter brought a small step-ladder, and this delighted Patty beyond measure.

"Ho!" said she, "now I'm 'Jack and the Beanstalk.' 'A-hitchet, a-hatchet, a-up I go'!" and with two jumps and a spring she landed in the upper berth.

"Now," she said to herself, "I know how Alice felt when she grew so large that she filled up the whole room. Let me see, what did she do? She put one arm out the window and one foot up the chimney. Well, I can't do that, and I don't see any little cakes to eat, as she did, that will make me grow smaller, so I s'pose I'll just have to scrounch around till I'm ready for bed, and then slide in. I'm sure I shan't sleep, it's all so noisy and exciting."

But when she finally straightened herself out on the coarse, cinder-sprinkled linen of the Pullman, the chink-a-chunk of the train changed to a lullaby, and in about two minutes Patty was sound asleep.

# CHAPTER III

IT was about four o'clock the next afternoon when the train came puffing into the great train-shed in Jersey City.

It had passed through Elmbridge about an hour before, but being an express train, it made no stop at such small places.

So Mr. St. Clair had arranged to meet Patty at Jersey City and take her back home with him.

Patty recognized her uncle as soon as he entered the car, and ran to greet him.

"Howdy, Uncle Robert," she said, in her pretty southern way, "are you looking for me?"

"I am, if you're little Patty Fairfield. But you've grown so since I saw you that I think I shall have to ask for your credentials."

Patty laughed, and answered: "My credentials are that I remember the doll and the candy you brought me five years ago, and I just *know* you're my Uncle Robert."

" I am indeed, and I've come to carry you off to a lot of other admiring relatives."

Then Patty introduced Miss Powers, and after gathering up the various wraps and bags they all left the train.  Miss Powers was to cross the ferry to New York, so Patty and Uncle Robert escorted her to the ferry-boat and bade her good-bye, with many thanks for her kind care of the little girl during the journey.

Then Uncle Robert said : " Now we'll go out to Elmbridge as quick as we can skip, but first we must pick up Ethelyn, whom I left in the waiting-room."

" Oh, is Ethelyn here ? " cried Patty.  " I am so glad, I'm just crazy to see her."

Apparently Ethelyn was crazy too, for she flew at her cousin as soon as she entered the door.

" You dear thing ! " she exclaimed, " I'm so delighted to see you.  Oh, how pretty you are ! We'll be awfully good chums, won't we ? "

" I'm sure we shall," replied Patty, who was just a wee bit frightened by this dashing young cousin.

Ethelyn was about Patty's age, but somewhat shorter and decidedly less slender.  Her yellow ᴜair was not long, indeed it was cut evenly round just above her shoulders, but it was crinkled and fluffed out until her head had the contour of a yellow pumpkin.

A huge black hat with a wide rolling brim was perched on top of the yellow mop, and ornamented with feathers and shining buckles.

Both the girls wore dark blue suits trimmed with fur, but Ethelyn's was resplendent with wide lace-trimmed collars, and she wore clattering bangles on her wrists, and a fancy little muff hung round her neck by a silver chain.

Her skirts were as short as Patty's, and she seemed like a little girl, and yet she had a wise, grown-up air, and she began to patronize her cousin at once.

"Your frock is nice," she said, "but it has no style to it. Well, I suppose you couldn't get much in the way of dressmakers where you lived, but Madame Marsala will soon turn you out all right. Mamma says she'll just enjoy ordering new clothes for you, and your papa told her to get whatever she chose. Oh, won't we have fun! We always go to New York for our things, and the shops are just lovely."

" Come, come, children," said Uncle Robert, who had been looking after Patty's trunks, " the train is made up, let us get aboard."

They went through one of a whole row of little gates in an iron fence, and Patty wondered at the numerous trains and the crowds of people moving swiftly towards them.

She wondered if everything at the North were conducted on such a wholesale and such a hurrying plan. They hurried along the platform and hurried into a car, then Uncle Robert put the two children into a seat together, while he sat behind them and devoted himself to his evening paper.

The girls chatted gaily and Patty learned much about the home she was going to, and began to think of it as a very beautiful and attractive place.

The train stopped at Elmbridge, and without waiting for her father, Ethelyn piloted Patty off the car.

" Here's our carriage," she said, as a handsome pair of horses with jingling chains came prancing up. A footman in livery handed the young ladies in, and Patty felt as if she had come among very grand people indeed.

While they waited for Mr. St. Clair, who was giving the checks to the baggage-master, Patty admired the pretty little station of rough gray stone, and the neatly kept grounds and paths all about it.

"Yes, they are pretty," assented Ethelyn, "but just wait till you see our grounds. We have the finest place in Elmbridge. In summer it's just lovely."

Then Mr. St. Clair came, and giving the coachman the order "Home," he seated himself opposite the two girls.

"Well, Patty, how do you like it, so far?" he asked, genially, of his niece.

"Oh, Uncle Robert, I think it's beautiful, but I hoped we'd have a sleigh-ride. I've never been in a sleigh."

"Bless you, child, we don't have much sleighing. However, perhaps we can scare up a sleigh-ride before the winter is over. We have a pretty fine sleigh, eh, Ethelyn?"

"Yes, indeed, we have a beautiful great big one, and I have a little cutter, all my own. I'll take you sleighing, Patty, if we get half a chance."

Soon they reached the St. Clair home and drove up the long winding avenue to the house.

Patty saw a brilliantly lighted mansion, and as they drew near it, she heard the most piercing shrieks and yells, as of a human being in desperate straits of some kind.

Patty wondered if she were about to enter a Bluebeard's castle, but deeming it polite to take no notice of the uproar, she tried to appear unheeding though the shrieks increased in violence as they came up to the house and the carriage stopped at the front door.

# CHAPTER IV

### VILLA ROSA

" HERE we are, chickens," said Uncle Robert, as the footman threw open the carriage door, " here's your new home, Patty, and you're very welcome to your Uncle Robert's house."

It was almost dark and Patty could distinguish only the outlines of a magnificent house, so large that it seemed like a palace.

They went up massive stone steps between great stone lions, to a wonderful veranda bright with electric lights, and lights streamed from every window and from the wide front doors which flew open as they reached them.

But though all this beauty and elegance impressed Patty like a dream of Fairyland, she paid little heed to it, for she was so shocked and disturbed by the shrieks from within, which were now distinctly audible as those of a child.

" Goodness me ! " exclaimed Ethelyn, just as Patty could stand it no longer and was about to

ask what it meant, " what can be the matter with
Florelle this time ?   I hope you enjoy squealing,
Patty, for you'll hear plenty of it in this house.
Don't mind it; little sister has a fearful temper,
and we have to let her squeal it out."

Patty was relieved to learn that it wasn't a
case of intentional torture, and by this time she
found herself in the great hall.

The grandeur of her surroundings fairly
dazzled her, for Patty was an inexperienced little
girl, and had lived simply, though very comfortably all her life.   And so she looked with amazement on the walls frescoed in brilliant colors, the
enormous gilt-framed mirrors, the tall palms and
marble statues, the rich draperies and stained-
glass windows.

If she had been older and more experienced
she would have known that it was *too* gorgeous,
the coloring too bright and garish, and the ornamentation over-showy.   But to her childish eyes
it all seemed wonderfully fine.

" Oh, Uncle Robert," she cried, " is this your
home ?   How beautiful it is !   I never saw such
a lovely place in my life."

This speech pleased Mr. St. Clair beyond

measure, for he dearly loved to have his beautiful home appreciated, and he beamed, and rubbed his hands together with a general air of satisfaction.

" Yes, yes," he said, " it is fine,—*fine !* There isn't another such place for miles around."

Then they went into the drawing-room and Patty was presented to her Aunt Isabel.

Mrs. St. Clair was a fair, large woman, with golden hair, elaborately frizzed, and kind blue eyes. She was fashionably dressed, and her silks rustled and her bugles tinkled as she came forward to meet her visitor.

" I am charmed to see you, Patty, my dear," she said, kissing her affectionately.

" And I am very glad to be here, Aunt Isabel," said Patty, and just then she was interrupted by the violent entrance of what seemed to be a small pink cyclone.

This was the eight year old Florelle, and without a doubt it was she who was responsible for the shrieks Patty had heard.

The child wore a short, beruffled dress of pink silk, a huge pink sash, and pink stockings and slippers. Her eyes were reddened with crying

and her cheeks were tear-stained, and she ran to
Patty, screaming:

" I will! I *will !* She's *my* cousin, and I'm
going to see her *now*."

Then she threw her arms round Patty's waist,
and smiled up into her face. She was a very
pretty little girl when she smiled, and Patty
couldn't help admiring her, though so far she had
seemed like anything but a lovable character.

" Oh, Florelle," said her mother, mildly, " how
naughty you are. I told you to go to bed like a
goody girl, and you should see Cousin Patty in
the morning."

" But I wanted to see her to-night. So I made
nurse dress me, and I'm going to stay up to dinner."

" Let her stay, mamma," said Ethelyn. " If you
don't, she'll yell again, and I'm tired of hearing
her."

" Yes, you can stay, baby," said Mrs. St. Clair,
" and now, Ethelyn, take Patty to her room, and
get yourselves ready for dinner."

The two girls went off together, and Patty
discovered that the rest of the house was as
sumptuous as her first view of it.

The same brilliant coloring and florid ornamentation appeared everywhere, and when at last Ethelyn stopped before an open door, and said, "This is your room," Patty gave a little cry of delight, for she entered what seemed a veritable fairy bower.

The walls and ceiling were tinted pink and frescoed with garlands of roses and flying birds. There was a fascinating bay window with latticed panes, and a cozy window-seat with soft cushions. The brass bedstead had a lace coverlet over pink silk, and the toilet-table had frilled curtains and pink ribbons. There were silver-mounted brushes and bottles and knickknacks of all kinds. The little work-table was a gem, and there was a lovely writing-desk with silver appointments and pink blotting-paper. Then there was a cozy divan, with lots of fluffy pink pillows, and through a half-opened door, Patty could see a dear little dressing-room.

There were beautiful pictures on the walls, and costly vases and bric-a-brac all about, and it all showed such kind thought on the part of somebody, that Patty's heart was touched.

"Is it for me? Who did it all?" she asked, turning to Ethelyn with shining eyes.

" Oh, mamma did it; she loves to do such things. That is, she planned it, and the servants did the work. Here's my room right next. It's just like it, almost." So it was, or at least it had been, but it showed signs of carelessness and disorder. A lamp globe was broken, and there was a large hole burned in one of the pretty rugs. The toilet table, too, was in sad disarray, and some papers were sticking out of the closed desk.

" Don't look at it," said Ethelyn, apologetically, " I'm so careless. I broke that globe when I was swinging my dumb-bells, and I've done it so often that mamma declared she wouldn't get me another. And I upset the alcohol lamp on the rug. But I don't care ; when we have a party it will all get spruced up ; mamma has everything put in order then. Now we'll dress for dinner, Patty. What are you going to wear ? "

" I don't know; I haven't many dresses. Aunt Isabel is going to buy me some, you know."

" Yes, I know. Let's see what you have."

Ethelyn was already kneeling before Patty's open trunk, and overhauling her belongings.

" Oh, here's a blue crape," she cried, " you must look sweet in this. Put it on."

" Why, that's my best party-frock, Ethelyn."

" Never mind ; wear it to-night, and mamma'll get you some new party clothes."

So Patty put on the blue crape, and very becoming it was, though somewhat inappropriate for a quiet family dinner.

" We only have one maid between us," explained Ethelyn, calling from her own room into Patty's. " Elise will do your hair when you want her, but just now she's doing mine."

To Patty's surprise, when she saw Ethelyn again, she was arrayed in a light green silk dress, and her hair was puffed high on her head. Patty wore hers as usual, and felt as if her cousin had suddenly grown up away from her.

" Doesn't my hair look nice ? " asked Ethelyn, as the girls went down-stairs together. " Mamma says I'm too young to have it done up this way yet, but I don't care what she says. I'm fifteen, and I think I'm old enough to do as I choose. To-morrow we'll make Elise do yours up and see how you look."

" But I'm only fourteen," protested Patty,

" and I don't want to be grown up for years yet. Your hair looks lovely, but I like you better with it down, as it was this afternoon."

" Don't say so before mamma, or she'll insist on my wearing it so."

When the girls entered the drawing-room, Mrs. St. Clair smiled amiably at her pretty niece, and bade her come to her side.

" My dear," she said, " you are a pretty little girl, and a sweet one, I've no doubt, but your name I do not like at all. I can't abide nick-names, so I'm going to call you by your full name. What is it, Martha? "

" Martha ! " exclaimed Patty in surprise, " oh, no, Aunt Isabel, I was named for my great-grandmother. My name is Patricia."

" Oh, how lovely," cried Aunt Isabel, kissing her niece in the exuberance of her delight. " We will all call you Patricia. It is a beautiful name and suits you extremely well. You must stand very straight, and acquire dignified manners in order to live up to it."

This made merry Patty laugh, but she offered no objection to her aunt's decision, and promised to sign her name Patricia whenever she wrote it,

and to make no further use of the despised nickname while staying at Villa Rosa. Ethelyn was
pleased too, at the change.

" Oh," she said, " now your name is as pretty
as mine and Florelle's, and we have the prettiest
names in Elmbridge. Here comes Reginald,
you haven't seen him yet."

Reginald St. Clair, a lad of thirteen, advanced
without a trace of shyness and greeted his new
cousin.

"So it is Patricia," he said, as he took her
hand; " I heard them rechristening you. How
do you do, Cousin Patricia?"

" Very well, I thank you," she replied, smiling,
" and though I meet you the last of my new
cousins, you are not the least," and she glanced
up at him, for Reginald was a tall boy for his
age, taller than either Ethelyn or Patty.

" Not the least in any way, as you'll soon find
out if you stay with us, Cousin Patricia."

Patty almost laughed at this boastful assump-
tion of importance, but seeing that the boy was
in earnest, she humored him by saying:

" As the only son, I suppose you *are* the
flower of the family."

Then dinner was announced, and the beautiful dining-room was a new pleasure to the little visitor. She was rapidly making the discovery that riches and luxury were very agreeable, and she viewed with delight the handsome table sparkling with fine glass and silver.

" Well, Patricia," said Uncle Robert, who had been warned against using the objectionable nickname, " how do you like Villa Rosa so far ? "

" Oh, I think it is beautiful, Uncle Robert. Every room is handsomer than the last, and my own room I like best of all. You're awfully good, Aunt Isabel, to give me such a lovely room, and to spend so much thought and time arranging it for me."

" And money, too," said her aunt, smiling. " That rug in your room, Patricia, cost four hundred dollars."

" Did it really ? " said Patty, with such a look of amazement, almost horror, that they all laughed.

You see, Patty had never been used to such expensive rugs, still less had she been accustomed to hearing the prices of things mentioned so freely.

" Oh, Aunt Isabel, I'd rather not have it then. Really, I'd much rather have a cheaper one. Suppose I should spoil it in some way."

" Nonsense, my dear, spoil it if you like, I'll buy you another," said Uncle Robert, grandly.

" Never mind rugs," interrupted Reginald. " I say, mother, aren't you going to give a party for Patricia ? "

" Yes, I think so," answered his mother, " but I haven't decided yet what kind of an affair it shall be."

" Oh, have a smashing big party, and invite everybody."

" No, Reginald," said Ethleyn, " I hate those big parties, they're no fun at all. It isn't going to be a party anyway. It's going to be a tea. Didn't you say so, mamma ? A tea is a much nicer way to introduce Patricia than a party."

" Ho, ho," laughed her brother, " a tea ! why they're the most stupid things in the world. Nobody wants to come to a tea."

" They do so," retorted Ethelyn, " you don't know anything about society. Teas are ever so much stylisher than evening entertainments, aren't they, mamma ? "

" Well, I don't know," said Mrs. St. Clair, doubtfully, " the Crandons gave a tea when their cousin visited them."

" Ho, the Crandons," sneered Ethelyn, " they're nobody at all; why, they've only got one horse."

" I know it," said her mother, " but they're awfully exclusive. They won't speak to hardly anybody."

" Then don't speak to them," said Mr. St. Clair. " I just guess we're as good as the Crandons any day in the week. I don't know as you'd better invite them, my dear."

" They wouldn't come if you did," said Reginald.

" They would so," snapped Ethelyn, " they'd jump at the chance."

" I bet they wouldn't ! "

" I bet they would ! You don't know everything in the world."

" Neither do you ! "

" Hush, children," said Mrs. St. Clair, mildly, " your Cousin Patricia will think you very rude and unmannerly if you quarrel so. Florelle is the only one who is behaving nicely, aren't you, darling ? "

Florelle beamed at this, and looked like a little cherub, until Reginald slyly took a cake from her plate.

" Oh-h-h ! " screamed Florelle, bursting into tears, " he took my cakie, he did,—give it to me ! " and she began pounding her brother with her small fists.

But Reginald had eaten it, and no other cake on the plate would pacify the angry child.

" No, no," she cried, " I want that same one, —it had a green nut on it,—and I wa-a-ant it ! "

" But brother can't give it to you, baby, he's eaten it," said her father, vainly trying to console her with other dainties.

But Florelle continued to scream, and Mrs. St. Clair was obliged to summon the nurse and have her taken up-stairs.

" Well, that's a relief," said Ethelyn, as the struggling child was carried away. " I told you you'd hear her yell pretty often, Patricia."

Patty felt rather embarrassed, and didn't know what to say; she was beginning to think Villa Rosa had some thorns as well as roses.

After dinner, as they sat round the great fire-place in the library, Mrs. St. Clair announced:

" I have made up my mind. I will give a tea for Patricia in order that she may be properly introduced to the Elmbridge people,—the best of them,—and then later, we will have a large party for her."

This pleased everybody and amiability was restored, and all fell to making plans for the future pleasures of their guest.

When Patty went to her room that night, she was so tired out with the excitements of the day, that she was glad to go to rest.

But first of all she opened the little box that her father had given her at parting. Was it possible that she had left her father only the day before? Already it seemed like weeks.

With eager fingers she broke the seals and tore off the paper wrappings, and found to her great delight an ivory miniature of her mother.

She had seen the picture often; it had been one of her father's chief treasures, and she prized it the more highly as she thought what a sacrifice it must have been for him to give it up, even to his child.

It was in a Florentine gold frame, and Patty

placed it in the centre of her dressing-table, and then sat down and gazed earnestly at it.

She saw a sweet, girlish face, which was very like her own, though she didn't recognize the resemblance.

" Dear mother," she said softly, " I will try to be just such a little girl as you would have wished me to be if you had lived to love me."

# CHAPTER V

### A MINUET

" MAMMA," said Ethelyn, the next morning at breakfast, " I'm going to take a holiday from lessons to-day, because Patricia has just come, and she doesn't want to begin to study right away."

" Indeed, miss, you'll do nothing of the sort," replied her mother; " you had a holiday yesterday because Patricia was coming; and one the day before, on account of Mabel Miller's tea; and you had holiday all last week because of the Fancy Bazaar. When do you expect to learn anything?"

" Well, I don't care," said Ethelyn, tossing her head, " I'm going to stay with Patricia to-day, anyhow; if she goes to the schoolroom, I will, and if she don't, I won't."

" Oh, I'll go to school with you, Ethelyn," said Patty, anxious to please both her aunt and cousin if possible.

But Mrs. St. Clair said, " No, indeed, Patricia, you don't want to begin lessons yet. Why, you're scarcely rested from your journey. I am going to New York to-day to buy you some new dresses, and if you're not too tired, you may go with me and help select them."

" Well, I just guess Patricia won't go to New York, unless I go too," cried Ethelyn in great excitement. " Do you think I'll stay at home and grub in the schoolroom while she's having a good time in the city? Not much, my Mary Anne!"

" Ethelyn!" said her mother, reprovingly, " how many times must I tell you not to use slang? It is vulgar and unladylike, and quite out of keeping with your social position."

" I don't care; it's expressive if it isn't stylish."

" Don't say stylish, either. That isn't genteel at all. Say ' correct.' "

" Oh, ' correct.' Well, mother, I guess it must be correct to use slang, 'cause Gladys Mahoney does, and she's a hummer on style."

" And I've no doubt her mother reproves her for it, just as I do you. Now go to the schoolroom, it is nearly ten o'clock."

"I won't go unless Patricia comes too. If she's going to New York with you, I'm going."

"Ethelyn," said Mrs. St. Clair, sternly, "do as bid you. Go to the schoolroom at once, and study your lessons diligently."

"No, I won't," replied Ethelyn, stubbornly, "I won't stir a step unless Patty comes too."

"But I'm going to take Patricia to New York."

"Then I'm going to New York," said Ethelyn, with an air of settling the question, and then she began drumming on the table with her fingers.

"I want to go to New York with you, mamma," said Florelle; "I want to buy a new dolly."

"No, baby," said her mother, "you can't go this time. You stay at home like a good girlie, and I'll bring you a beautiful new doll."

"But I *want* to go! I *will* go!" and Florelle began to cry.

"Stop that crying," said her father, "stop it at once, and when I come home I'll bring you a big box of candy."

"No, I don't want candy,—I want to go to New York,—I want to go—I do-o-o," she wound up with a prolonged wail.

"Good gracious, Florelle," said Reginald, "do

stop that fearful yowling. If you don't, as soon
as I go down town I'll send a bear back here to
eat you up."

At this Florelle screamed louder than ever, and
had to be taken away from the table.

Patty felt quite helpless in the midst of this
commotion. She had been accustomed to obey
willingly her father's lightest wish, and Ethelyn's
impertinence amazed her. As for little Florelle,
she thought the child was quite old enough to be
reasoned with, and taught not to cry so violently
over every trifle.

But she realized it was not her place to criti-
cise her cousins' behavior, so she did the best
she could to pour oil on the troubled waters.

"Aunt Isabel," she said, "if you don't mind,
I'll stay at home and study with Ethelyn."

"Well, do as you like, child," said her aunt,
carelessly; "of course I can select your clothes
just as well without you, and I'll take you both
to New York some Saturday. But you needn't
study unless you choose, you know."

"Well, I'll stay with Ethelyn, anyway," said
Patty, tucking her arm through her cousin's as
they went off to the schoolroom.

"What a mean old thing you are," said Ethelyn crossly. "You might just as well have said you'd go to New York, and then I would have gone too, and we could have had a lovely time shopping, and lunching at Delmonico's, and perhaps going to a matinée."

"But your mother said you couldn't go," said Patty, in surprise.

"Oh, that's nothing. I would have gone all the same, and now you've spoiled it all and we've got to drudge over our books. Here's the schoolroom. Miss Morton, this is my cousin, Patricia Fairfield. She is to begin lessons to-day."

While Ethelyn was talking, the girls had mounted to the third floor of the great house, and entered the large and attractive-looking schoolroom.

Miss Morton was a sweet-faced young woman, who greeted Ethelyn pleasantly and then turned cordially to the stranger.

"We are glad to have you with us," she said; "you may sit here at this desk, and presently I will ask you some questions about your studies."

Reginald was already in his place and was studying away for dear life. He was naturally a studious boy, and he was anxious to prepare himself to enter a certain school the next year.

But Ethelyn had no taste for study, and she flounced herself into her chair and unwillingly took up her books.

" Now, Ethelyn," said Miss Morton, " you must learn that history lesson to-day. You've dawdled over it so long, that it has become a real bugbear to you. But I'm sure if you determine to conquer it, you can easily do so. Just try it."

" Ho," called out Reginald, teasingly, " can't learn a history lesson! I couldn't wait for you, so I went on ahead. I'm 'way over to the ' Founding of the German Empire.' Where are you in history, Patricia ? "

" I've only studied United States History," she replied, a little ashamed of her small attainments, " but I've been through that twice."

" Well," said Miss Morton, kindly, " it's better to know one thing thoroughly than to have smatterings of a great many. If you are familiar with United States History, you will enjoy lessons in the history of other countries for a change."

" I'm sure I shall," said Patty, " and my father told me to study whatever you thought best for me. But I don't like to study very much; I'd rather read story books."

Miss Morton examined Patty in arithmetic, geography, and some other branches, and decided that as her attainments in knowledge were about equal to those of her cousins, they might all have the same lessons each day.

Patty afterwards discovered that Reginald learned these lessons, and Ethelyn did not. But she simply skipped them and went on to the next, apparently making the same progress as her brother.

Patty had become absorbed in her history lesson, which was very interesting, when Ethelyn began to chatter.

"Miss Morton," she said, "we are going to have a party for my cousin."

"Are you? That will be very nice, but don't let us discuss it now, for I want you to put your whole attention on that history lesson."

"I will,—but, Miss Morton, it's going to be a very grand party. Everybody in Elmbridge will be invited. I mean," she added, tossing her head, "everybody that *is* anybody."

"Everybody is somebody," said Reginald.

without looking up from his book, " and I wish you'd keep still, Ethelyn."

" Well, you know what I mean; everybody that's rich and important, and fit for us to know."

" Why," said Patty, looking at her cousin in surprise, " aren't people fit for you to know unless they're rich ? "

" No," said Ethelyn, " I wouldn't associate with people unless they were rich, and neither would you, Patricia."

" Yes, I would," said Patty, stoutly, " if they were good and wise and refined, and they often are."

" Well, you can't associate with them while you're living with us, anyhow; we only go with the swells."

" Ethelyn," said Miss Morton, gently, " that isn't the right way to talk. I think —— "

" Oh, never mind what you think," said Ethelyn, rudely, " you know the last time you preached to me, I nearly made mamma discharge you, and I'll do it for sure if you try it again."

Miss Morton bit her lip and said nothing, for she was a poor girl and had no wish to lose her lucrative position in the St. Clair household, though her ideas were widely at variance with those of her employers. But Patty's sense of justice was roused.

" Oh, Ethelyn," she said, " how can you speak to your teacher so ?   You ought to be ashamed of yourself."

" Oh, Miss Morton don't mind, do you ? " said Ethelyn, who was really only careless, and had no wish to be unkind, " and it's true.  I will have her sent away if she preaches at us, 'cause I hate it ;  but she won't preach any more, will you, Morty ? "  and Ethelyn smiled at her governess in a wheedlesome way.

" Go on with your lessons," said Miss Morton, in a quiet tone, though she was with difficulty repressing a desire to tell her pupil what she thought of her.

" Yes, do," growled Reginald ; " how can a fellow study when you're chattering away with your shrill voice ? "

" I haven't got a shrill voice," retorted Ethelyn, " have I, Patricia ?  Mamma says a soft, low voice is very stylish,—correct, I mean, and I'm sure mine is low and soft."

Ethelyn said this in such an affected whisper that Patty had to smile.

But Reginald said:

"Pooh, of course you have when you put on airs like that, but naturally your voice is a cross between a locomotive whistle and scratching on a slate."

"It isn't!"

"It is!"

"Well, yours isn't a bit better, anyway."

"I didn't say it was, did I?"

"I didn't say you did say so, did I?"

"I didn't say you said I said so, did I?"

"I didn't say you said, I said—you said, ——"

"Children, stop quarreling," said Miss Morton, half laughing at the angry combatants whose flushed faces showed signs of coming tears.

But Patty laughed outright. "What sillies you are," she said, "to squabble so over nothing."

When school was over, it was time for luncheon, and after that Ethelyn told Patty that it was the afternoon for dancing-class and they were all to go.

"You must wear your blue crape, Patricia."

she said, " and make yourself look as pretty as you can, and put on all your jewelry."

" But I haven't any jewelry," said Patty; " papa says little girls oughtn't to wear any."

" No jewelry? Why, how funny. I have loads of it. Well, no matter, I'll lend you some of mine; or we'll crib some out of mamma's jewel-case; I know where she hides the key."

" Thank you, Ethelyn, but I wouldn't wear borrowed ornaments, and I don't want to wear jewelry anyway. I'm not old enough."

" Oh, you are too! what silly, old-fashioned notions you have. And besides, while you're with us, mamma said you must do whatever we want you to."

So Patty reluctantly allowed Ethelyn to clasp a necklace round her throat, and slip several jingling bangles on her wrists.

" There! " said Ethelyn, adding an emerald brooch, which she had selected from her mother's collection, " now you don't look like a pauper, anyhow."

" But I don't feel comfortable, Ethelyn, and besides, suppose I should lose these things."

" Oh, you won't lose them; and if you should,

I don't believe mamma would scold much.
She'd like it better than if I let you go looking like a nobody, and have the Mahoneys think
our cousin was poor."

Ethelyn herself was resplendent in red silk
trimmed with spangled lace. She wore shining
slippers with high French heels, and all the
jewelry she could cram on to her small person.

Florelle looked like a fairy in a short little
white frock, all fine muslin and lace, with ruffles
and frills that stood out in every direction. The
overdressed little midget was delighted with her
appearance, and pranced around in front of the
mirror admiring herself. Reginald too, considered himself very fine in his black velvet suit,
with a great white collar and immense white silk
tie.

Miss Morton accompanied the children, and
the St. Clair carriage carried them away to the
dancing class. When they arrived, all was bustle
and excitement. About forty gaily dressed
children were assembled in a large hall, prettily
decorated with flags and flowers.

Patty was fond of dancing, and danced very
gracefully in her slow, Southern way, but she

was utterly unfamiliar with the mincing steps and elaborate contortions attempted by the Elmbridge young people. However, she enjoyed it all from its very novelty, and she was pleasantly impressed with some of the boys and girls to whom she was introduced.

But she was amazed and almost angry at the way her cousin talked about her.

"Mabel," said Ethelyn, as she presented Patty to Mabel Miller, "this is my cousin, Patricia Fairfield. She is from Richmond, Virginia, and is visiting us for the winter. Her father is a millionaire, and he has lots of great plantations of,—of magnolias."

"Oh, no, Ethelyn," began Patty.

"Well, sweet potatoes, then, or something," went on Ethelyn, nudging her cousin to keep still. "You must excuse her dress, she couldn't get anything very nice in Virginia so mamma has gone to New York to-day to buy her some decent clothes."

Patty raged inwardly at this slighting and unjust remark about her native state, but she was a truly polite little girl and said nothing unkind in reply.

"Do you like to dance?" said Mabel Miller to Patty later, as they took places in a quadrille just forming.

"Yes," said Patty, "and I know these quadrilles, but I never saw fancy dances like those you have here."

"Oh, they're the latest thing," replied Mabel. "Professor Dodson comes from New York, and he teaches us the newest and swellest steps."

As that day was the last of the quarter the professor had arranged a little exhibition of his best pupils, and a good-sized audience was gathered in the galleries above the dancing floor to witness it.

But it was a surprise to all present when he announced that a friend whose name he was not privileged to mention, had offered a prize to the child who should dance most gracefully, either alone or with a partner.

"You can't get it, Ethelyn," said Reginald, "for you're as awkward as a lame elephant."

"I am not," snapped Ethelyn, "and you'd better not try for it, 'cause you'd only make a spectacle of yourself."

"So would you," retorted Reginald, "and then we'd be a pair of spectacles."

Ethelyn said no more, for the dances were beginning.

Some of the pupils danced very prettily, others affectedly, and others cleverly, but the dances were of a kicking, romping nature that required much practice and skill to perform gracefully.

After all had taken part, Professor Dodson turned politely to Patty, and invited her, if she would, to dance also.

"Oh, I couldn't, thank you," she answered. "I don't know any of these flings. I only know an old-fashioned minuet."

"Try that," urged Ethelyn, who delighted to have her cousin made conspicuous, as that attracted attention towards herself.

The professor insisted upon it, so Patty obligingly consented, and saying, "I couldn't dance with these things jingling," she gave Ethelyn the heavy necklace and bangles.

Then she stepped out on the floor, and as the orchestra played the slow, stately music of the minuet, Patty bowed and swayed like a veritable old-time maiden. Graceful as a reed, she took the pretty steps, smiling and curtseying, her fair little face calm and unflushed.

It was such a pretty dance and such a contrast to the acrobatic, out-of-breath performances of the other dancers, that, without a dissenting voice, the committee of judges awarded the prize to Miss Patricia Fairfield.

Patty was delighted, for she had no idea that her dancing was specially meritorious and she accepted the gold medal with a few words of real gratitude, thinking the while how pleased her father would be, when she should write him all about it. On the way home she said to Ethelyn :

" But it doesn't seem right for me to have this prize, as I'm not a member of the dancing class."

" Oh bother," said Ethelyn, " that doesn't matter; they're always giving out prizes, and I'm awfully glad you got this one. People will think you're something wonderful. And I'm sure they'd have given it to Belle Crandon if you hadn't danced, and mamma will be tickled to death to think you got it ahead of her."

# CHAPTER VI

## PURPLE AND FINE LINEN

WHEN Mrs. St. Clair's purchases were sent home from New York and spread out on view, Patty could scarcely believe her own eyes.

Were all those fine clothes really meant for her?

The materials included silks, satins and velvets in bright colorings and somewhat conspicuous patterns.

Some of the dresses were already made up, and these were befrilled and beflounced, with lace and embroidery. As Patty had always worn delicate shades of material, and her dresses had been very simply made, she couldn't help protesting at all this bewildering array of finery. But her aunt said:

"Nonsense, child, you don't know what you're talking about. You are the guest of the St.

Clairs, and your appearance must do us credit.
I am not giving you these things, you know;
your father wrote me to buy for you whatever
was necessary or desirable.   I have a lot of new
clothes for Ethelyn, too, and I want you to look
as well as she does.   While you are with us you
must be suitably dressed, else I shall feel ashamed
of your appearance."

Poor Patty began to wonder whether it was so
very nice after all, to have fine clothes if she
could have no voice in their selection.

But she thought, what is the use of objecting?
Aunt Isabel will do as she pleases anyway, and
while I'm staying with her, I ought to agree to
what she wants.

Then two dressmakers came to stay a fort-
night.   Ethelyn and Patty were given a holiday
from lessons, the schoolroom was turned into a
sewing-room, and Miss Morton and Reginald be-
took themselves to the library.

Patty was rather sorry to miss her school
hours, for the history lessons had become interesting, but she soon found that Aunt Isabel's
word was law.   It was a law often broken by her
own children, but Patty was not of a mutinous

heart, and she amiably obeyed Mrs. St. Clair's commands.   But she had her own opinion of the household, and she did not hesitate to express it plainly in her letters to her father.

" I begin to see," she wrote to him one day, " what you meant when you explained to me about proportion.   In this house, money, and fine clothes, and making a great show, are out of all proportion to everything else.   They never think of reading books, or doing charity work, or anything but showing off.   And if a thing costs a lot, it's all right, but if it's simple and not expensive, it's no good at all.   I can tell you, Mr. Papa, that when we have our home, we'll have less fuss and feathers, and more comfort and common sense.   And it isn't only that the things cost so much, but they're always talking about it, and telling how expensive they are.   Why, Uncle Robert has told me half-a-dozen times how much his horses and carriages cost, and now he says he's going to get an automobile, so I don't know what he'll do with his horses.   Ethelyn is very nice in some ways, but she is affected and rude, and I don't like her as well as Clara Hayden, if she *is* my cousin.   Reginald is a

nice boy, but he's sort of pompous and con-
ceited, and thinks he's better than any one else in
the world.  Little Florelle is a dear, but she
cries so easily that I can't have much fun with
her.  But there, now I've told you all the bads,
I'll tell you some of the goods.  Miss Morton,
the governess, is a lovely lady, and when Ethelyn is so cross I can't stand her, I go to Miss
Morton, and we have a walk or a drive together,
and have nice, pleasant talks.  And then I am
taking singing lessons twice a week.  Aunt
Isabel says I have a pretty good voice, and I
love to sing, and Reginald takes me skating, and
that is splendid.  I don't know how yet, but he
says I am learning pretty well.  Aunt Isabel
gave an afternoon tea for me, and next week we
are going to have a big party, and I think that
will be nice.  I like parties and dancing-school,
only the girls and boys all act so grown up.
They are about my age and even younger, and
they act as if they were ladies and gentlemen.
That isn't good proportion, is it?  But I am
pretty happy, except that I am often homesick
for you.  Then I look at your picture, and at the
beautiful picture of dear mamma and it helps

some.　And your letters help me too, so write just as often as you can, won't you?

" From your loving daughter,
" PATRICIA FAIRFIELD."

The party, as Patty had feared, was a very grown-up affair. For several days beforehand the servants were getting the house ready for it, and all was bustle and confusion.

The furniture and bric-a-brac were all removed from the hall and drawing-room and library, and carried up to the third floor to be out of the way. The portières were taken down from the doorways, and on the day of the party they were replaced by simulated curtains of smilax and flowering vines.

As it was near the Christmas season, the decorations included evergreens, holly and mistletoe, but besides these, quantities of roses and rare flowers of all sorts were used. The florists came early and worked all day, and they transformed the house into a fairy bower.

Patty was delighted with this, and walked through the luxurious rooms, quite lost in admiration of their floral beauty.

Carpenters had enclosed the great veranda which was then hung with red satin and decorated with ropes and wreaths of holly, and, like the rest of the house, was fairly ablaze with electric lights.

The party was to be from eight to twelve, and when Patty went down-stairs at a little before eight, she found her uncle berating the musicians, who were a little late in arriving.

" I want you to understand," Mr. St. Clair was saying, " that when *I* send for you, you are to come when I bid you. Don't tell me you couldn't help it,—if there is danger of detention on the road, you should start earlier. *I* am accustomed to having *my* orders obeyed, and all who are employed at Villa Rosa must fully understand that. Go on with your music, and next time, see to it that you arrive more promptly."

Uncle Robert strutted away with such a pompous air, that Patty was almost afraid of him herself. But when he saw her, he beamed kindly, and said :

" Come here, my dear, and tell me what you think of all this."

" I think the house looks beautiful, uncle, just

like Fairyland, with all the flowers and lights.
And I think you are very kind to give this party
for me."

" Well, well, child, we have to invite our
friends occasionally, you know.   Have a good
time, and I shall feel amply repaid for my out-
lay.   Those American Beauties are fine, aren't
they ? "

" Indeed they are," said Patty, sniffing at one
that reached its rich redness temptingly towards
her.

"Oh, don't do that !   You'll spoil them.
Those roses cost six dollars a dozen.   But how
fine you look in your new gew-gaws.   Turn
round, little one.   Ah, we have no reason to feel
ashamed of our Southern maid to-night."

Patty was glad her uncle was pleased, for she
herself felt rather uncomfortable.   Her dress,
which was made with low neck and short sleeves,
was of red silk gauze, with multifold short skirts,
accordion-plaited, and edged with thick, full
ruches.   Great golden butterflies were embroidered at intervals all over the dress, while ribbons and flowers were attached wherever a place
could be found for them.

Ethelyn had coaxed Patty to have her hair dressed high on her head, so Elise had arranged a marvelous *coiffure* which displayed jeweled pins and combs of many sorts, and a necklace and bracelets rivaled them in glitter. Red silk stockings, and red satin slippers with gilt butterflies on them completed this gorgeous costume, and when Patty saw herself in the long mirrors, she thought she looked like one of the paper fairies which she used to hang on her Christmas trees.

When the party began, she stood beside her aunt and Ethelyn and received the guests as they arrived.

About fifty boys and girls came, and to Patty they all seemed like overdressed and artificial little puppets.

The girls put on grown-up airs, walked with mincing steps and giggled behind their fans, while the boys were affected and absurdly formal.

Patty had thought there would be games or amusements of some youthful sort, but dancing and promenading alternated throughout the evening.

However, she was fond of dancing, and as she

was quickly becoming a general favorite, her card was soon filled with the names of the nicest boys in the room.

It was all very pleasant for a short time, but soon Patty grew very tired and secretly longed for supper to be announced.

At last this came to pass, and the children marched out to the dining-room where another beautiful sight awaited them.

The caterers had been as skilful as the decorators, and the table was filled with marvelous confections of rich foods.

Patty had never seen such wonderful things, and she almost thought the pheasants were alive; and the big salmon looked as if it had just been taken from the water. Then there were salads and croquettes, and funny little paper dishes filled with strange, delicious mixtures, and after all these, came creams and jellies and ices, and cakes and bonbons in all sorts of odd shapes and colors.

Patty thought these things were too pretty to be eaten, but they were quickly demolished by the young people, who were hearty, hungry boys and girls, in spite of their affected manners.

After supper the dancing and promenading began again, and was kept up until midnight, and Patty was a very tired little girl after she had said good-night to all the guests and the last carriage had rolled away from Villa Rosa.

Ethelyn was tired too, and decidedly cross.

" I didn't have a very good time," she said; " that horrid old Gladys Mahoney had a prettier dress than mine; and I broke my new fan, and my slippers are so tight, they hurt me awfully."

" Pooh, I know what makes you cross," said Reginald, " just 'cause Bob Burton didn't dance with you as much as he did with Mabel Miller."

" I'm not cross," retorted Ethelyn, " and I didn't want to dance with Bob Burton. If I were you, I'd try to learn some manners; Lou Smith says you're the rudest boy she ever saw."

" I don't care what Lou Smith says,—little, freckle-faced thing! I don't see why she was invited here, anyway."

" Stop quarreling, children," said Mrs. St. Clair, " and go to bed at once. Patricia, I hope you enjoyed the party; I'm sure I tried to have it nice, but everything seemed to go wrong.

The salad wasn't fit to eat and the ice cream was half melted."

"Why, Aunt Isabel," said Patty, "I think everything was lovely. I never saw such a supper-table in my life, and the decorations were exquisite."

"Well, I didn't think so. It does seem a shame to pay out so much money, and then not have things to your liking."

"Oh, the party was good enough," said Mr. St. Clair, "you're too fussy about trifles, Isabel. Come, children, scurry off to bed, you'll get no beauty sleep to-night, I fear."

Patty went to her room, and taking her mother's picture, sat down to talk to it, as she did nearly every night.

"Motherdy," she said, "if you had lived to take care of me, I don't believe you'd have liked the party we had to-night. The grown-upness of it was all out of proportion for children, I think, and,—as usual in this house, the expense was out of proportion to everything else. Why, Uncle Robert must have spent a thousand dollars for it,—maybe more,—he'll probably tell us to-morrow just how much everything cost. I liked some of the party,—the supper was lovely, but, —well, I reckon I ate out of proportion too. You see, little mother, it's very hard always to do just right.  Now I'm going to bed, and I'm so sleepy, I don't know as I'll wake up before to-morrow afternoon."

She kissed the beautiful face, and putting the picture back where it belonged, she hopped into bed and was soon fast asleep.

# CHAPTER VII

## A SLEIGH-RIDE

THE winter slipped away, and as Patty was a little girl who always looked on the bright side of things, she really had very good times at Villa Rosa.

She became a favorite with the Elmbridge boys and girls, and her unfailing good nature kept her from quarreling with her cousins, though she was often sorely tried by them.

Lessons were a very uncertain quantity. Sometimes there would be none at all for a week or two weeks, and then perhaps school would keep regularly for a few days, only to be followed by another interruption.

Patty found it only too easy to fall into these careless ways, and if she had stayed all her life at Villa Rosa, I fear she would have become indolent and selfish, for the rule of the whole household seemed to be "Pleasure before Duty," and when that rule is followed it often happens that the duties are not done at all.

In January, to Patty's great delight, there came a heavy snowstorm.

It made fine sleighing, for the roads were in just the right condition and as the weather was clear and cold there was good prospect of many days' fun.

Uncle Robert, always ready to give the young people a good time, instigated a sleighing parade, in which all the society people of Elmbridge were invited to join.

It was to be a grand affair. Every sleigh was to be decorated in beautiful or unique fashion, and there was great rivalry among the families of Elmbridge as to whose sleigh should present the finest spectacle.

"Papa," said Ethelyn, "I shall drive Patricia in my little cutter, of course, and I want you to fix it up, somehow, so that it will beat everybody else all hollow."

"Ethelyn," said her mother, "if you don't stop using those slang phrases, you shan't go in the parade at all. Now promise to talk like

a lady, and I'll see to it that your sleigh out-
shines all the rest."

"All right," said Ethelyn, "I'll promise.
Now, how shall we decorate it?"

"Never mind," said her mother, "I wouldn't
trust you with the secret. You'd tell everybody
before the parade, and give them a chance to
imitate it. But just wait and see. You and
Patricia shall drive the most beautiful turnout in
the whole line."

That day Mrs. St. Clair made a hurried trip
to New York and came home with many mys-
terious packages, and other larger packages
came by express. Mr. St. Clair came home
early from his business and spent much of his
time in the barn, and the preparations grew so
exciting that both Patty and Evelyn were on tiptoe with curiosity and anticipation. The parade
was to start the next afternoon at two o'clock.
Soon after luncheon, Mrs. St. Clair sent the girls
to their rooms to dress for the great event.

Ethelyn gave a little scream of delight, as she
saw new garments spread out on her bed, and
Patty ran on to her own room to find similar
ones there.

Each girl had a long coat of fine white broad-cloth, made with a double cape-collar, and trimmed all round with white fur. A broad-brimmed white felt hat, with white ostrich plumes and a fleecy white feather boa, white gloves, and a white muff were there too; and even white shoes and white cloth leggings, so that when the cousins were dressed, there was not a touch of color about them, save their rosy faces and golden hair, and they looked like veritable snow-queens.

They danced down-stairs to find Cupid awaiting them with a brand-new sleigh.

Cupid was Ethelyn's pony, and he was pure white, every bit of him, and it was this fact that had suggested the whole scheme to Mr. St. Clair.

The new sleigh was pure white too, trimmed here and there with silver.

Cupid's harness was all white and silver, and waving white plumes and silver bells were in various places about the sleigh and horse.

There were big white fur robes, and when Mr. St. Clair tucked the girls in, and Ethelyn took the white reins and white whip, it certainly seemed as if no sleigh load could be prettier.

And none was. Everybody agreed that the white sleigh was the pride of the parade. Patty secretly wondered why her aunt was satisfied without more gaudy coloring; as she wrote to her father afterwards, she had half expected to see a red sleigh with blue and yellow robes. "But," she said, "I suppose it was because Cupid happened to be white, and I'm glad he was, for it was all just lovely."

Mr. and Mrs. St. Clair and Florelle went in the parade also, but they contented themselves with the family sleigh, which of course was both handsome and elaborate. They had spent all their energies on the girls' appearance and they were very proud of the result.

Reginald, who was of an ingenious turn of mind, had contrived an affair which was supposed to look like a Roman chariot, and which was, therefore, a bit incongruous on runners.

It was very fancy, being almost entirely covered with gilt paper, and it had two wheels and no back. It jolted fearfully, and Reginald was occasionally thrown out. However, he stuck to it pluckily, until his machine was a total wreck, when he abandoned it, and jumped into his father's sleigh for the rest of the parade.

Patty enjoyed it all hugely. It was such a novel experience to fly along, through the crisp, cold air, and over the shining snow roads; and Ethelyn was in such jubilant good-humor, that the whole affair marked a red-letter day in the winter calendar.

The " White Flyer " was the talk of the town for weeks after, and Mr. St. Clair never tired of telling any one who would listen, how much it all cost, and how difficult it was to get the white sleigh and harness on such short notice.

Patty grew very tired of this pompous boasting, and, notwithstanding her enjoyment of the luxury at Villa Rosa, she was not altogether sorry when the time drew near for her to go away to Boston to make her next visit.

She was to leave the St. Clairs about the first of March, and spend the next three months with her father's sister, Mrs. Fleming.

As Uncle Robert was her mother's brother, the two families were entirely unacquainted, and the St. Clairs could tell Patty nothing about the new home to which she was going.

" But," said her Aunt Isabel, " I feel sure you won't like them as well as you like us. Are they rich, Patricia ? "

" I don't know," answered Patty; " papa never said anything about that. He said that they are a very literary family."

" Humph," said Aunt Isabel, "then I guess they haven't very much money ; literary people never do have. Poor child, I suppose they'll turn you into a regular little blue-stocking."

Patty didn't relish this idea, for at Villa Rosa she had fallen into the habit of neglecting her lessons, and already study was losing its charm for her. But she was fond of reading, and she felt sure she would enjoy an atmosphere of books.

On the 14th of February, Aunt Isabel gave a party for the young people, which was a farewell party for Patty, though it was also a festival in honor of St. Valentine's Day.

As usual, the girls had new dresses, and they represented Mrs. St. Clair's idea of valentines.

Ethelyn's was of blue, and Patty's of pink silk, and they were trimmed with innumerable lace flutings and garlands of flowers. They were further decorated with gilt hearts pierced by darts, and with skilfully made artificial doves which perched on the shoulders of the wearers.

The party was a very pretty one, as Aunt Isabel's parties always were.

The rooms were decorated with roses and pink ribbons, and gilt hearts and darts, and feathered doves and wax cupids. At supper the ices and cakes were heart-shaped, and after the children had returned to the drawing-room St. Valentine himself appeared.

As Patty suspected, it was Uncle Robert dressed up to represent the old Saint, with flowing white hair and beard and a gilt paper halo. He wore a long white robe with red hearts dotted all over it, and carried a gilt bow and arrow.

He carried also a pack or pouch full of valentines which he distributed to the guests.

Of course they were very handsome affairs, and in each was hidden some dainty trifle, handkerchief, fan or bonbons.

Besides those at the party, Patty received numerous other valentines, some of which came by mail, and others in the good old-fashioned way, under the front door.

Many of these were from the Elmbridge young

people, while several from Richmond included a
beauty from her father, and a pretty one from
Clara Hayden.

Although the cousins had varying tastes, they
had become very good friends, and both felt sad
when the day came for Patty to leave Villa Rosa.

Indeed, the whole family felt sad, for Patty
was a very lovable little girl, and had endeared
herself to them all.   Uncle Robert was to take
her to New York and put her on the boat, where
Mr. Tom Fleming would meet her and take her
to his mother's house in Boston.

Aunt Isabel said she, too, would go to New
York with Patty, and of course Ethelyn announced her intention of going.

Then Florelle set up such a howl to go, that
Patty begged her aunt to take her, and the child
went.

Reginald declined to be left out of such a family affair, so Patty was  amply escorted to her
destination.

They went on board the *Priscilla*, a beautiful
boat of the Fall River Line, and Mr. St. Clair
soon found Mr. Fleming, who had agreed to
meet him at a certain spot.

Then Patty was introduced to her Cousin Tom, who was a tall young man of about thirty-five, with a pointed beard, and dark, pleasant eyes.

"So this is my little Southern cousin," he said, cordially, as he took her hand.

Then he chatted affably with the whole party until the warning gong announced that they must go ashore.

Ethelyn was heart-broken at the thought of parting, and flinging her arms round Patty's neck, burst into tears.

This was enough for Florelle, who promptly followed suit, and set up one of her very best howls.

With a good-bye kiss to his niece, Uncle Robert picked up the screaming child and marshaled his family off of the boat, and Patty was left alone with her new-found cousin.

# CHAPTER VIII

## AN ABSENT-MINDED COUSIN

"Now, Patty," said Cousin Tom, as they walked along the saloon, "I am going to hand you over to the stewardess, who will show you your stateroom. Go with her, and she will look after you. I think you would better leave off that heavy coat, as it is too chilly outside to permit of going on deck, and the atmosphere within is quite warm. Ah, here she is. Stewardess, this is Miss Fairfield and here is her stateroom key. See to it that she is made comfortable."

As Mr. Fleming supplemented his request with a pecuniary argument, the stewardess made Patty her especial charge, and assiduously looked after her comfort.

"And, Patty," said her cousin, as she turned away, "when you are ready, come back and you will find me right here. See, just by this staircase. Lock your door and bring the key with you."

Patty felt as if she had suddenly grown several years younger, for Cousin Tom talked to her as to a little child. " It's more like Wonderland than ever," she said to herself. " Only instead of growing big or little, I grow old or young. At Aunt Isabel's I was considered a young lady, but Cousin Tom seems to think I'm a small child."

The stewardess, who was a good-natured old colored woman, took Patty to her stateroom, and then helped her to unpack her traveling-bag, and arrange her belongings for the night.

As Aunt Isabel had bought her clothes, of course Patty was absurdly overdressed.

When she took off her blue velvet coat with its ermine collar, her blue silk, lace-trimmed dress looked far more suitable for a grand reception than for traveling.

" Laws, missy," said the voluble stewardess, " how handsome you is ! "

Patty thought this a reference to her dress, but the remark was meant for the child herself, whose flower-like face looked out from a most becoming big hat of plaited blue velvet, and her golden hair fell in a loosely tied bunch of long thick curls.

When Patty returned to her Cousin Tom, she found him sitting just where he said he would be, but so deeply absorbed in a book that he did not see or hear her approach.

Not wishing to disturb his reading, she sat down in the large chair next to him and waited.

She didn't mind this at all, for it was very interesting to watch the people passing up and down, and the saloon itself was beautiful to look at. Patty sat for a long while, but Cousin Tom never moved, except to turn the pages of his book. She did not like to speak to him, as she feared he would think it necessary to lay aside his book and entertain her; she had no wish to trouble him, and beside, she was quite capable of entertaining herself.

So after she had sat still for a long while, she decided to walk about the cabin a bit, always keeping in sight of Cousin Tom, if he should raise his eyes. But he didn't, and Patty strayed farther and farther away from him, until she had explored all the available parts of the boat.

She was much interested in all she saw, and many admiring eyes followed the pretty, graceful child as she walked about.

When she reached the dining-room she looked in, and the sight of the passengers sitting at well-filled tables made her feel very hungry, and she wondered if Cousin Tom would finish his book in time to give her any dinner. Somehow she felt sure he never would look up until he *had* finished the book.

She went back and sat down again beside him with a little sigh. But he didn't hear the little sigh, and kept on reading.

Patty looked at him curiously. There was little hope of his finishing the book, for he was only about half-way through it, and he read very slowly, turning the pages at long intervals. She could see his eyes move eagerly along the printed lines, as if delighted with what he found there.

She waited a while longer, and then said to herself, " I don't care, I'm going to speak to him. I've waited a million hours, and the dinner will be all eaten up."

She didn't speak, but she rose and stood by his side, and then with a sudden impulse she laid her hand with outspread fingers upon the page he was reading.

Cousin Tom jumped as if a firecracker had exploded in his vicinity, and he looked at Patty with a dazed expression.

" Bless my soul ! " he said, " why, little one, I forgot all about you.    Will you forgive me ? Have you been here long ?   I was reading, you see, and I didn't hear you come."

" I've been here an hour, Cousin Tom," said Patty, demurely.

" An hour ?   No!   Is it possible ?   You poor child, why didn't you tell me ? "

" Oh, I didn't mind," said Patty, " and you seemed to be all wrapped up in your book."

" Yes, I was,—I was.    But I'll try to make amends.   Come, let's go and have some dinner."

Taking Patty's hand, Cousin Tom strode along the saloon, and down the stairs, and Patty almost had to run to keep up with his long steps.

" Now," said he, as they seated themselves at a table and an obsequious waiter began to put ice and then water into their glasses.   " Now, what would you like to eat ? "

" Oh, anything at all," said Patty, gaily, " I'm hungry enough to eat,—I don't know what."

" Yes, yes, of course you are,—poor child,—so sorry I forgot you,—quite inexcusable of me."

Mr. Fleming was looking over the bill of fare as he talked, and then he looked doubtfully at Patty, as if uncertain what he ought to order for her.

" What would you like for your dinner, child? Now don't say you don't care, or that you'll leave it to me, for little girls always say that, and I declare I don't know what you ought to have."

" All right," said Patty, who was quite equal to the occasion. " Let's have some lobster mayonnaise, and some mushrooms under glass, and little tiny clams, and tutti-frutti and a Dewey Punch."

Cousin Tom stared at her in amazement.

" What are you talking about?" he exclaimed; " you'd be dead if you ate all those things. Are they on the bill of fare? What is a ' Dewey Punch '?"

" Oh, I don't die so easily as that. Ethelyn and I used to eat worse mixes than that, whenever we lunched at the New York restaurants. A Dewey Punch is a lovely kind of ice cream with strawberry jam or something poured all over it. I don't see it on the list; perhaps they don't have it. Never mind, we'll take meringue glacé."

"Indeed we won't. I've changed my mind and I'll order this dinner myself. You shall have some soup, a broiled chicken, some vegetables and a plain ice cream. There, how do you like that?"

Cousin Tom didn't speak crossly at all, but very decidedly, and there was a pleasant twinkle in his eye that took away all idea of censure, so Patty said, amiably:

"I think it will be very nice and I really don't care what we have, only you told me to suggest something, so I did."

"Certainly, that's all right, but your suggestions were suicidal. Are you familiar with Bacon?"

Oh, thought Patty, he's going to order the breakfast over night, and I hate bacon.

"Yes," she said, "but I don't like it at all."

"You don't? What a perverted taste. But Boston will soon change that. We have a Bacon club, which you shall join. It is a most delightful club, and you will like it, I'm sure. I fancy that in a few weeks I shall see you devouring Bacon with intense enjoyment."

Indeed I won't, thought Patty. She was about to say that her Uncle Robert belonged to a Terrapin Club, but refrained, thinking it might be impolite to imply disparagement to the more lowly bacon.

So she changed the subject, and said:

" Please, Cousin Tom, tell me something of your family. It's so queer to go to see people and not know anything about them beforehand. But so far, my relatives have been very nice."

" Oh, the Flemings are a wonderful family," said Cousin Tom, gaily, " we are all going to do something great, but somehow we haven't hit it off yet."

" Cousin Elizabeth is an author, isn't she?" inquired Patty, a little timidly, for she had never seen a real, live author.

" Yes," said Mr. Fleming, " Elizabeth is an author, that is, she writes novels when she isn't doing anything else; Barbara is a club woman, but she writes too, more or less."

" And what do you do? Are you literary?"

"Yes, I'm writing a book, myself. It's a treatise on The Will, and I flatter myself I have some novel theories; and then there's Ruth, you know."

"Ruth, who is she?"

"Oh, she's our cousin, who lives with us. Not your cousin, you know. She is father's brother's child, and her people live in the country; so, as she has a fine mind, she lives with us in order to have the advantage of a Boston education."

"How old is she?" asked Patty.

"Fourteen or fifteen, I think. She'll be company for you; I think you'll like her, though she is very different from you."

"What is she like?" asked Patty, much interested in this new and unexpected comrade.

"Why, she is quiet, and very studious, and— but you'll see her yourself, to-morrow, so I'll let you form your own opinion."

After dinner they had a short promenade on deck, but the wind was so strong, that Patty was glad to return to the warm, light saloon, and they sat down on one of the red velvet sofas. Cousin Tom didn't resume his book, and Patty felt that he was politely trying to entertain her.

So with a desire to entertain him in return, she asked him to tell her about the book he was writing.

This seemed to please him immensely, and he eagerly launched into a description of its scope and plan.

As the subject was far above Patty's comprehension, she listened without understanding it clearly at all, and after a half hour or so, the continuous conversation, and the soothing motion of the boat caused the little girl quite unintentionally to fall sound asleep.

Mr. Fleming kept on talking for some time after this, when suddenly it occurred to him that his cousin sat very still, and peering round the corner of the big blue velvet hat, he discovered that his audience was quite oblivious to his learned discourse.

At first he looked a little annoyed, then he smiled compassionately, for the tired child seemed to be very peacefully resting, and her pretty head made a lovely picture against the red velvet sofa.

Mr. Fleming sent for the stewardess, and then awoke the little sleeper.

" Come, Patty," said he, gently tapping her on the shoulder, " it's bedtime, little girl, and you must run away to your bunk.'"

Patty opened her eyes and stared about her.

" Oh, Cousin Tom," she said, as she remembered the circumstances under which she had fallen asleep, " I'm *so* sorry,—I didn't mean to go to sleep, and I *was* interested."

" That's all right, my small cousin," said Mr. Fleming, " and now go along with the stewardess, and go to sleep and get a good night's rest." Patty did as Cousin Tom directed, and never wakened until she heard the steamer scraping against the dock early the next morning.

She rose and dressed quickly, and when the stewardess came for her, she was quite ready to go to meet Cousin Tom, who awaited her in the cabin.

" I shall give you a roll and a cup of coffee," he said, as if half afraid that Patty would want to order unheard-of dishes, " for they are expecting us home to breakfast, and we have only fifteen minutes before our train starts for Boston."

Patty drank her coffee and ate her roll with a

relish, and declared herself ready to start. A short ride in the cars brought them to Boston. They left the train and entered the waiting-room, where Cousin Tom placed Patty in a seat, and told her to stay there and not move while he attended to her trunks.

Patty obediently sat still, and soon she saw Cousin Tom returning. But just before he reached her, he met a man whom he evidently knew, and whom he seemed overjoyed to meet. The two men talked earnestly together, and then both turned and walked away.

Patty had seen instances of her cousin's absent-mindedness, even since he had neglected to take her to dinner the night before, and she guessed at once that he had forgotten her existence, and was going away with his friend.

She had no intention of being deserted in this way, so she left the bags and wraps which she was supposed to be guarding, and ran after him.

"Cousin Tom!" she cried as she caught up with him, "where are you going?"

"Bless my soul!" he exclaimed, staring at her, "I forgot you were with me. What shall I do? Allow me to present Mr. Harding. Ted, this is

my cousin, Miss Patty Fairfield; I am supposed to be escorting her home, but if what you tell me is so, I must go at once to see Varian. Wait, I have it, Patty; I'll send you home by a messenger; you don't mind, do you?"

"No, indeed, Cousin Tom," said Patty; "send me any way you like."

So Mr. Fleming called a messenger-boy, and giving Patty, and all the wraps and bags into his charge, he sent them to his mother's house. "Tell them I met Harding, and had to go away with him on some very important business," he said to Patty. "I'll be home to-night,—good-bye."

And with a hasty hand-shake, he turned again to his friend and they walked rapidly away.

"Come this way, miss," said the messenger, who was a tall youth, polite and deferential, and who appeared not at all surprised at the order given him. "I'll take you along all right."

He piloted Patty with great care and after riding for some distance on the street cars, they arrived at Mrs. Fleming's house.

# CHAPTER IX

### THE FLEMINGS

THE messenger-boy rang the door bell, and a white-capped maid opened the door. When she saw the uniformed youth, she held out her hand for his book, signed it and dismissed him.

Then turning to Patty, she said, " This way, miss," and ushered her into a small reception room.

As Patty wrote to her father afterwards, she felt like a package sent from a department store, and she looked down, almost expecting to find herself wrapped in paper and tied with a string.

After she had waited about ten minutes, a tall young woman came quickly down-stairs and passed along the hall. She had on a hat and jacket, and was evidently going away in a great hurry.

As she went by the reception room, she

caught sight of Patty through the open door, and stopped in surprise.

"Good-morning," she said, in a quick, hurried way. "Did you wish to see me?"

"I don't know," said Patty, uncertain whether this was a cousin or a visitor at the house. "I am Patty Fairfield."

"Oh, yes, of course,—our cousin from the South. I'm so glad to see you,"—she shook Patty's hand hastily,—"but I must ask you to excuse me this morning, as I am just going to a meeting of the 'Current Events' Club, and I am already five minutes late."

With an apologetic smile she hastened away, and Patty waited again.

Then she heard another step on the stairs, and another lady entered the room. This time it was Aunt Hester. She was a delicate looking little woman with silver hair, but Patty knew her at once from her resemblance to her father, who was Mrs. Fleming's brother.

"My dear child," said her aunt, as she kissed Patty, affectionately, "we are very glad to have you with us. But where is Tom?"

"He met a friend, Mr. Harding, and went

away with him on very important business. He said to tell you he would be home to-night, and he sent me here by a messenger-boy."

"Very well; I am glad you reached here safely. Are you hungry? Have you breakfasted?"

"I had coffee and rolls on the boat, but I *am* hungry," said Patty, frankly.

"Of course you are; well, you shall have something to eat. Let me look at you. Yes, you do look a little like brother Fred. How old are you?"

"Fourteen," replied Patty.

"Ah, just the age of Ruth Fleming, who lives with us, and who will be pleasant company for you. I hope you will be happy with us, my dear, and you mustn't mind being left to yourself a bit, for we are very busy people. Life is too short to be wasted in idleness."

"Yes," assented Patty, thinking that this aunt was indeed very different from Aunt Isabel.

"And now," continued Mrs. Fleming, "I am going to send Molly to you, and she will show you to your room, and afterwards give you some breakfast. I must ask you to excuse me this

morning, as I have to go to the sewing-class.
Ruth is at school, but we will all meet at luncheon which is served promptly at one."

Mrs. Fleming went away, not hurriedly, but
with a quick, decided step, and in a few moments
Molly, the maid appeared.

She was a merry-looking Irish girl, and her
pleasant smile was such a contrast to the pre-
occupied manners of the ladies, that Patty felt
friendly towards her at once.

" Come with me, Miss Fairfield," she said, and
taking up Patty's hand-luggage, she led the way
to a room on the third floor. It was a good-
sized room, very neat and well-furnished, but
with none of the luxury and beauty of Patty's
room at Villa Rosa.

There was a square dressing-table and exactly
in the centre of it was a square pincushion, with
a glass toilet bottle on either side and behind it
a smaller glass bottle to match. The chairs were
stiff and straight, and there was a haircloth sofa
with a small, square pillow at each end and one
in the middle.

In the centre of the room was a table with
books on it, and writing materials, and a

drop-light hung over it from the chandelier above.

Though plain in its appointments, the room was light and airy and exquisitely neat and well-kept.

Molly deftly unfastened Patty's bag and shawl-straps, and then said:

"Now, miss, I'll go below, and when you're ready, come down three flights of stairs to the dining-room, and I'll give you some breakfast."

Patty thanked her, and when she had left the room, Patty sat down in the small, straight-backed rocking-chair to "think herself out," as she sometimes expressed it.

She felt a little homesick for the warm-hearted friends at Villa Rosa, and yet she felt sure her Boston relatives were going to be very nice, if only they could ever find time to talk to her.

She wondered if the ladies were always hurrying off to club-meetings, and if Ruth were always studying. She would be glad when Cousin Tom came home, for she was very sure she liked him.

She looked critically at her surroundings and decided that when her trunks came, and she

could put the pretty things that she owned all
about, the room would look much more cozy
and attractive, and so, though her reception had
chilled her a little, she thought that perhaps she
would have a good time in Boston after all.

She jumped up and began to arrange such
things as she had brought with her.

Her pretty silver brushes and trays looked
somewhat out of place on the prim dressing-
table, but Patty thought them a decided improvement. Then she unwrapped her mother's
portrait, and placed it on the writing-table.

" It's a funny place, this, motherdy," she whispered to the picture, " and I don't know whether
we'll like it or not; but we'll be happy together,
you and I. And I think we'll like Aunt Hester, for she's papa's sister, you know, so she
must be nice."

Then Patty went down the three flights of
stairs, as directed, in search of Molly.

" It's funny," she said to herself, " to go down
cellar to breakfast. But I'm sure she said three
flights," and sure enough, when she reached
the basement, Molly met her with a kindly
smile, saying,

"Come this way, miss," and Patty found that the front basement was the dining-room.

Its large windows were protected by iron railings, and the whole room had an air of solemn dignity rather than cheerfulness, but Molly was so pleasant and cordial that Patty felt cheerful at once.

The smiling Irish girl brought her some fruit, an omelet, hot rolls and delicious coffee, and after she had finished her solitary meal, Patty felt better able to cope with whatever might be awaiting her.

But apparently, nothing awaited her.

It was about ten o'clock, and as luncheon was announced for one, Patty wondered what she was expected to do in the meantime.

She asked Molly where Miss Elizabeth Fleming was.

"Laws, miss," said Molly, rolling her eyes, "don't make no attempt for to see her. She's writin' a novel, and she's up in her den on the fourth floor. We don't even call her to her meals. If she wants to come, she comes; and if she don't, I takes a few things up and sets 'em outside her door."

"Oh," said Patty, with great interest, "can't you speak to people when they're writing novels?"

"Indade, no, miss. It spiles the whole thing, and they has to begin all over again if a word is spoken to them."

"I think that's wonderful," said Patty, much impressed, "and I'm just crazy to see my Cousin Elizabeth. And Ruth, where is she?"

"Miss Ruth, she's at her school, miss, around on the next block. She'll be home at one o'clock and then you'll see her. Now why don't ye go and lie down and rest yerself?"

"But I'm not tired," said Patty, "I just want to get started; get to living here, you know. Can't I go into the library and look at some of the books?"

"Yes, miss, sure, if there's nobody there. I'll shlip up an' peep."

Molly went softly up-stairs, and Patty followed on tiptoe. It seemed strange to be so quiet, for at Villa Rosa everybody seemed to try to make all the noise possible.

"You can go in," said Molly, after her peep, "nobody's there; but the chairs is all settin' in rows, so I guess a club or somethin' is comin'. But go in, miss, dear, an' amuse yerself."

So Patty went in the library, which was a large back room on the main floor.

It has been said that a house without a library is like a body without a soul, and surely the library was the soul of the Fleming home. It was a beautiful room, built out behind the rest of the house, with a large skylight of stained glass, and a wide bay window whose cushioned seats looked very attractive.

Patty sat down and looked about her. The room was furnished with many well-filled bookcases, several small desks and tables, and a number of reading-chairs, whose broad arms held books and magazines.

Patty began at once to examine the titles of the books, and was delighted to find a large case full of children's books, containing all her old favorites, and many more that she had never read.

She selected "The Water Babies," which belonged to the latter class, and curling herself up on the window-seat, was soon absorbed in the story.

A little later, she heard the street door open and shut, and then Cousin Barbara whisked hurriedly into the library. She didn't see Patty at first, but sat down at a desk at the other end of the room, and hastily sorted over some papers.

"Ten-thirty to eleven-thirty, pigs," she murmured; "eleven-thirty to twelve, write paper on Choctaw costumes; twelve to one, attend Bootblacks' dinner. Ten-thirty! Why it's time for the pigs now."

"Will I interfere with the pigs if I stay here, Cousin Barbara?" said Patty, curious to see the animals appear, but not wishing to intrude.

"What! are you there, Patty? Yes, you may stay if you like, but make no noise or disturbance of any kind."

"I won't," said Patty, and then Miss Barbara proceeded to ignore her small cousin's presence, and in her hurried way, prepared her books and papers, and laid small slips of paper and pencils in various chairs, and occasionally jotted down something in a small note-book which she took from her pocket.

Soon several strange ladies were ushered into

the room by Molly, and Patty was much disappointed by the fact that they brought no pigs with them, and was just hoping that they would arrive later, when the meeting was called to order, and she learned that it was a committee from the Town Improvement Association, to consider ways and means for the amelioration of the general condition of the Common Pig.

Patty thought this was very funny, and wanted to laugh when the ladies discussed it seriously and with great enthusiasm. Sometimes several talked at once, and then Cousin Barbara rapped on her desk with a little hammer and they began all over again.

At half-past eleven, they all went away, and Cousin Barbara whipped out her packets of papers once more. Then she selected several books from the shelves, and sat down to write. Presently she looked up, bewildered.

"Can I help you, Cousin Barbara?" said Patty, eager to be of assistance.

"No,—yes,—" said her cousin, absent-mindedly. "Yes—if you will please hand me the encyclopedia—the one labeled cho———"

Patty easily found the desired volume and

carried it to her cousin, who said, " Thank you," and then scribbled away as fast as she could until the clock struck twelve.

" Now," she said, thrusting her papers in her desk, " I must go to the Bootblacks' Dinner," and hastily putting on her jacket and gloves,— she had kept on her hat,—she flew out of the room, and almost instantly the street door closed behind her.

Then Patty resumed her book and read until one o'clock, when a great gong that could be heard all over the house announced luncheon.

Delighted at the thought of seeing the family at last, Patty skipped down-stairs.

Aunt Hester was in the dining-room and greeted her niece cordially.

" Well, my dear," she said, " I hope you found something to amuse you this morning. To-morrow, if you wish, you may go to school with Ruth. Ah, here she comes now. Ruth, this is Patty Fairfield, my brother's child, from Richmond."

" I am very glad to see you," said Patty pleasantly. " Cousin Tom told me you were here, and I hope we shall be good friends."

"I hope so," said Ruth, a little awkwardly, for she was a trifle confused by the graceful elegance of Patty's manner.

Ruth Fleming was a thin slip of a girl, with a very pale face, large gray eyes, and light brown hair which was smoothly brushed back, and tightly braided. She wore a gray dress and her whole effect was plain and colorless.

Her face was pure and intellectual, but so calm and expressionless that Patty wondered if she ever laughed aloud, and if she ever enjoyed herself very much in any way.

Ruth took her place at the table without another word, and Patty sat down beside her determined to make her say something, if she had to pinch her.

But just then Cousin Elizabeth came in, and Patty rose to greet her.

Miss Elizabeth Fleming was a large, handsome woman with black hair, and snapping black eyes, and such a winning smile that Patty liked her at once.

"Well, Patty cousin, have you come at last?" she said. "I've been waiting for you several years, and I'm very glad to see you." She gave

Patty an affectionate caress, and kept on talking
as she seated herself at the table.    Patty afterwards discovered that Cousin Elizabeth always
kept on talking, no matter what happened, or
who else was talking at the time.

" Yes," she said, " we've all wanted to see our
Southern cousin, and now that I have seen you,
I think you are delightful.    Mother, Geraldine
has been the hatefullest thing this morning ; she
just sat down on a blue satin sofa, and she
wouldn't move, nor she wouldn't say a word.    I
declare I've lost all patience with her."

" Who is Geraldine ? " said Patty, " is there any
one else in the family ? "

" Geraldine is the heroine of my new novel,"
said Cousin Elizabeth, " and she is lovely, but so
intractable.    You wouldn't believe how sulky
and stupid she gets at times.    Ah, Barbara," as
her sister bustled into the room, and dropped
into a chair at the table, " how are the bootblacks ? "

" Oh, they're lovely," said Barbara, " they ate
all the dinner, and then stole the forks.    I res-
cued some of them, though—Elizabeth, can't
you go to see the Common Council this after-

noon about that Statue Fund? I have a
Mothers' Meeting at two, and after that we re-
hearse the Greek pantomime, and oh, mother,
did you keep that Greek robe of mine, or did you
give it away?"

"I gave it to a peddler," said Mrs. Fleming;
"it was full of moth holes, and soiled besides.
He gave me two saucepans for it."

"Never mind, sis," said Elizabeth, "you can
borrow a Greek robe from Martha Fowler; she
has one, I know, and I'll stop there for it, as I
return from the Authors' Tea. Ruth, what have
you on hand for this afternoon?"

"I practice until three, Cousin Elizabeth.
Then 'The Golden Branch' from three till four,
and after that my French lesson and the Physical
Culture class."

"H'm, well,—somebody ought to entertain
Patty. Mother, what are your plans?"

"I have to go out to Cambridge this afternoon,
to collect for the Dorcas Aid Society. Patty
can go with me if she likes, but I'm afraid she
wouldn't enjoy it very much."

"No, I'll take Patty with me," said Cousin
Elizabeth, very decidedly. "She'll like the

Authors' Tea, I know, and if we have time, we'll look in at the Library."

When luncheon was over, they all flew away on their respective errands, and Cousin Elizabeth told Patty to put on her hat and coat, and meet her in the reception-room in ten minutes.

# CHAPTER X

## PATTY'S PRANKS

SOMEHOW the time passed quickly in Boston; in fact, the Fleming family seemed fairly to push it along, they hurried so.

At any rate they wasted none of it, and after a few weeks, Patty fell into the ways of the household, and hurried along with the rest.

Indeed she had to do so, or be left behind, for her cousins were like Time and Tide, and waited for no man, or little girl either.

She went to school with Ruth, but found herself far behind the New England girl in her studies, so she took her place in a lower class, and Ruth kindly helped her with her lessons at home.

Patty did not know what to make of Ruth; she had never seen a girl like her before. Of course Ruth was pleasant and amiable, but she was so very quiet, seldom talked and almost never laughed.

Patty joked with her, and told her funny stories, but at most she received only a faint smile in response, and sometimes a blank stare.

She wrote to her father : " Ruth is the queerest girl I ever saw, and I believe she is all out of proportion. She studies so hard that she has crowded all the fun out of herself. You know ' all work and no play makes Jack a dull boy,' and I verily believe Ruth is the dullest girl in the world."

But Ruth almost always won the prizes offered at school, and was accounted the best of Miss Goodman's pupils.

Patty liked the school, and she liked Miss Goodman, the principal, but the hours, from nine to one, seemed very long to her, and she would often get restless and mischievous.

One day she thought she would clean her ink well. Ruth shared her desk, and as the ink well was intended for the use of both, it was a good-sized one, and chanced to be full of ink.

So Patty must needs find something to hold the ink while she washed the inkstand. Not having anything appropriate, she made a cornucopia of a sheet of stiff writing-paper.

She turned up the point securely, poured the
ink in, and folded down the top, feeling sure that
she could get the ink well ready before the ink
soaked through the paper.

Ruth saw this performance and a look of grave
disapproval was on her face, but as communica-
tion of any kind during school hours was strictly
forbidden, she made no sign.

Just as Patty had completed her dangerous
little bundle, and held it in her hand, looking at
it admiringly, Miss Carter, the teacher, happened
to notice her.

Now as the strict discipline of the school pro-
hibited anything which was not directly an aid
to education, Miss Carter felt it her duty to con-
fiscate the suspicious-looking package, that *might*
be candy, and that certainly did not pertain to
school work.

"Patty Fa' ield," said she, in a commanding
voice, "you are out of order.   You have there
something apart from your school duties.   Bring
it to me at once."

"But, Miss Carter,"—began Patty.

"Silence! not a word! hand me that parcel

"Oh, Miss Carter, I can't! it's ——"

" One word more, and you will be expelled from school.   I require implicit obedience.   Bring me that parcel."

As there was really nothing else to do, Patty walked up to Miss Carter's desk, gingerly carrying the package of ink.

She knew what would happen if Miss Carter took it, but she had tried to explain, and as she was not allowed to do so, she couldn't help feeling that the result would serve the teacher right for being so unreasonably tyrannical.   But she thought she would attempt one more warning, so she said,

" You'll be sorry if you take it, Miss Carter."

Angry at what she considered an impertinent threat, Miss Carter grasped the paper of ink with an indignant clutch, and a black flood streamed over her hand and dress, and spurted out in various directions.

Some drops flew in her face, and on her immaculate white collar, while others decorated her desk and papers with black blots.

The pupils, who had watched the scene with interest, though only Ruth knew what was in the cornucopia, were horror-stricken at the calamity, and sat breathlessly awaiting the explosion of Miss Carter's wrath.

But a drop of ink rolled down that lady's august nose, and involuntarily she put up her hand to brush it away. This produced such an all-over smudge on the ink-spotted face that the girls burst into uncontrollable laughter, and the unfortunate teacher rushed out of the room.

Patty was not expelled from the school, for after hearing Ruth's grave and carefully exact version of the case, Miss Goodman decided that though Patty was blameworthy, yet Miss Carter had been too peremptory in her orders, and so had brought the trouble upon herself.

Patty, who was fun-loving, but not malicious, went to Miss Carter privately, and made her peace with the irate lady, but it was several days before the ink stains entirely disappeared from the teacher's face ; and as for the blots on the desk and platform, I shouldn't be surprised if they were there yet.

When Patty told about the ink episode at home, Aunt Hester was exceedingly shocked, but Cousin Tom said, " Patty, you're a genius. What made you think of wrapping up ink in paper ? "

" There was nowhere else to put it, Cousin Tom."

" I suppose if you hadn't had any paper you would have dumped it into your pocket, eh ? "

" Tom," said his sister Barbara, " how careless you are in your diction. ' Dumped ink ! ' One can only dump a powdered or granulated substance. By the way I've joined a new club. It's a Society for the Improvement of Advertisers' English, and we work in such a novel and efficacious way. To-day Miss White and I were appointed a committee to go through the shops in a certain district, and call attention to any errors which we noticed on signs or placards. Well, we went into a large dry goods house, and the first thing that caught my eye was a sign ' Dotted Swisses, twenty-five cents.' I sent for the advertising manager and he came. Then I said to him, ' Sir, this is a reliable house, and of course you advertise nothing that you cannot supply. A Swiss is a native of Switzerland, and experience has taught me that a Swiss is often an admirable servant, especially clever as a cook. So if you can sell me a Swiss for twenty-five cents, I'll take one, and I don't care whether he is dotted or not.' The man looked extremely mortified and stammered something about meaning muslin goods sold by the yard. 'Oh,' said I, 'if you mean dotted Swiss muslins, why don't you say so?' and Miss White and I stalked out of the shop."

"That club of yours is a good thing," said Mr. Fleming, meditatively, "I hope you will banish the signs which announce 'Boots Blacked Inside,' and those others which always rouse false hopes in the minds of people who have lost their umbrellas, by promising 'Umbrellas recovered while you wait.'"

"Yes, we will, and we're going to do away with those atrocious doggerel rhymes in the street cars and substitute real poetry. It will cost a great deal to get it written, but we have funds, and the public taste must be elevated."

The work of such clubs as this, and constant endeavors towards educational or literary attainment of one sort or another, engrossed the attention of the whole Fleming family.

Amusement or recreation not of a literary nature was never indulged in.

So serious were they in their aims and purposes, that all fun was crowded out, and to fun loving Patty this was a sad state of affairs indeed.

As she wrote to her father, " the worst kind of misproportion is that which leaves out all fun and jokes and laughing. And I'm going to play a joke on the whole family, if I can think of a good one, just to stir them up for once."

Then Patty tried her best to think of some hoax or trick that would be harmless, and yet would startle all the Flemings out of their usual busy routine.

As the first of April drew near, she did think of a plan, and she decided that April Fool's Day gave her a legitimate excuse for teasing her serious-minded relatives.

As a family, their habits were most methodical ; meals were served exactly at the appointed hours, and every one appeared in the dining-room as if by magic, punctual to the minute. Breakfast was at eight, and Patty had often heard Cousin Elizabeth say that she always woke on the stroke of seven. None of the others woke earlier than that, as a rule, and rules in the Fleming house had very rare exceptions.

So Patty decided to try a bold scheme, which was nothing less than to set everybody's clock two hours ahead on the morning of the first of April, and let the people waken to find they had apparently overslept.

She could not have managed this very well, except for the fact that Cousin Tom had remarked a few days before that he had left his watch at a jeweler's to be cleaned, and was carrying an old one which was very unreliable.

So mischievous Patty woke very early on the morning of the first of April. Indeed she had waked several times during the night, so anxious was she for the success of her trick.

As soon as the dawn made it light enough for her to see her way indistinctly round the house, she slipped on her dressing-gown, and crept softly down-stairs.

It was just half-past five by the old grandfather's clock in the hall, and Patty opened its glass door, and pushed the hands around until they stood at half-past seven. Then she went to the dining-room and kitchen, and changed those clocks to correspond.

The library clock was harder to manage, for it

was a cuckoo-clock, and she had to stand on a
table to reach it.

But Patty was a determined little girl, and having set out to fool the family she was not to be
baffled by small obstacles.   Then she went up
to the second floor and into her Aunt Hester's
room.   She felt a little bit like a burglar when
she saw the dear old lady peacefully asleep in
her bed.

But it was only the work of a moment to
change the time of the little clock that ticked
softly on the mantel, and then Patty slipped into
the next room.   Cousin Elizabeth's watch lay on
her dressing-table, and as it was a little stem-
winder just like Patty's own, it was easy to turn
the tiny hands two hours ahead.

Cousin Barbara's watch was under her pillow,
but as the sound sleep of that lady was pro-
verbial, audacious Patty slipped her hand under
her cousin's head, took out the watch, changed
the time, and replaced it, and Miss Barbara
Fleming slept on in blissful ignorance.

Patty was afraid that Cousin Tom would spoil
the whole joke.   But she knew that he had no
clock in his room, and only awoke when his

mother knocked at his door each morning. She hoped that in this case he wouldn't look at his watch, or if he did, he would have no faith in the uncertain old chronometer he was carrying at present, and anyway it wouldn't be believed against the testimony of all the other timepieces in the house.

Last of all, she slipped up to the servants' room and changed the time of their alarm clock.

Bridget, the cook, and Molly were sleeping, each in a narrow bed, and Bridget was snoring loud enough to wake them both, but she didn't.

Then Patty hurried back to her own room and jumped into bed again to await results.

Ruth had no clock or watch. She seemed to get up at the right time by instinct, and Patty, after carefully thinking it all over, concluded she had done her work very thoroughly.

And so she had,—and her trick was a great success. Of course the alarm clock went off apparently two hours late. Bridget woke with a start, looked at the clock, rubbed her eyes and looked again, and then she turned to Molly.

"Arrah, Molly," she cried, "will yez luke at that now. The alarrum is jist afther goin' off, an' it's eight o'clock! Whativer will happen to us?"

Molly jumped up in great excitement, and the two maids hastily dressed and ran down-stairs.

Of course it was really only six, but as the sun was now shining brightly, they had no thought for astronomical calculations, and besides, they were frightened nearly out of their wits. Such a thing had never before happened in the well-regulated Fleming household.

As no one was astir, they went on down to the kitchen, corroborating the time by the various clocks, but utterly unable so understand why the family were still all asleep.

Patty heard them whispering as they went down, and choking with laughter, she prepared to wait another hour for more fun,—and it came.

Elizabeth woke just at seven, and rising, glanced as usual at the watch on the dressing-table.

" Nine o'clock!" she almost screamed, running to her sister's door.

" Barbara! what does this mean? It's nine o'clock! Are you asleep?"

Barbara *was* asleep, but she awoke at her sister's call and drew her watch from beneath the pillow.

" It is," she cried, " it's nine o'clock! What shall I do? There's a rehearsal of the Historical Tableaux at ten, and I have to make three wigs before I go."

" But even that isn't as important as my engagement," wailed Elizabeth, who was splashing her face with water. " I have to be at the Authors' Club at nine-thirty, to prepare the room for the reception at eleven, and nothing can be done until I get there. And I must do several errands on my way there. Oh, it *can't* be nine o'clock. Perhaps my watch stopped at nine last evening. No—it's going. Oh, how unfortunate I am. Mother, mother," she called.

But Mrs. Fleming was already up, and came through the hall with a scared face.

" Girls," she said, " it's after nine o'clock, and Tom has to go away on the 9:45 train. We have overslept ourselves."

" I should think we had," began Elizabeth, but Mrs. Fleming had already gone to her son's room. " Tom, Tom," she called, as she knocked vigorously at the door, " get up, it's after nine o'clock ! "

" What ! " came from Tom's room, accompanied by a sudden jump out onto the floor.

Ruth had heard the commotion, and she and Patty each appeared at their doors.

" What is it, Aunt Hester ? " asked Ruth, roused at last, Patty was glad to see, to some degree of animation.

" Why, Ruthy, it's nine o'clock ! We have all overslept. Hurry down-stairs, children, you'll be late to school."

Well, such a commotion as there was ; everybody compared watches and clocks, and exclaimed in wonderment and dismay. Tom said that his watch said it was only half-past seven, but of course, as he had said it didn't keep perfect time, it was not believed, when all the others said half-past nine.

After they were all down-stairs and seated at the breakfast table, Patty remarked quietly,

" April Fool ! It isn't half-past nine at all ; it's only half-past seven. I set all the clocks forward two hours."

" What ! " said Cousin Elizabeth, looking as if

she would annihilate her. "You little witch! You dared to —" and then she felt such a relief to think she would have ample time to keep her engagement after all, that the ridiculous side of the affair struck her, and she began to laugh.

"Why, Patty Fairfield," said Barbara, and then she too laughed; and Cousin Tom, when he found he could catch his train, thought it all the best joke in the world.

Bridget and Molly enjoyed it the most of all, perhaps because, being Irish, they had a greater sense of humor than the Bostonians, but all agreed that Patty had played a very successful April Fool joke on them. All except Ruth,— she didn't see any fun in it at all, so Patty gave her up as a hopeless case.

# CHAPTER XI

### THE BOOK PARTY

ONE evening as they all sat in the pleasant library, Cousin Elizabeth announced her intention of giving a party for Patty.

" I am afraid," she said, kindly, " that you find it dull with us. We are all so busy with our club work and study, that we have really neglected your entertainment. I am sorry for this, and I mean to give you more youthful pleasures during the remainder of your stay with us."

Patty was delighted, for life at the Flemings *was* a little bit humdrum for her, though her aunt and cousins were very kind whenever they had time to remember her existence.

They all fell in with Elizabeth's plan, and began to discuss what kind of a party it should be.

Patty was secretly much amused at the contrast between plans for a party at Villa Rosa, and in Boston. Nothing was said about decorations.

and the supper was not mentioned, except when Cousin Elizabeth said she would order some cake and ice cream from a confectioner; and as to dresses, well, *they* seemed never to be even thought of by the Fleming ladies. Patty wore the plainest of the clothes her Aunt Isabel had bought for her, but even those were far finer than Ruth's.

Apparently the difference was not noticed, for no one paid the slightest attention to what any one wore.

The Fleming ladies were always dressed neatly and inconspicuously, but Patty concluded they must pick their dresses off of trees, for nothing was ever said about dressmakers or purchase of materials.

So when the party was talked about, all discussion was concerning the entertainment of the minds of the young guests.

Intellectual games were proposed, and even Ruth grew almost excited over the scheme of a " Quotation Salad."

But Cousin Elizabeth said, " Games are not enough. I want something more like a character party. Ah, I have it. Let us ask each guest to represent some children's book, or some favorite character in juvenile literature."

" Just the thing," exclaimed Barbara; " Eddie can be ' Little Lord Fauntleroy.' "

Eddie was a neighbor's child, who had long flaxen curls and who would make a perfect counterpart of the pictures of Fauntleroy. The Flemings all entered into the plan of the party with their usual enthusiasm, and found time between their numerous engagements to prepare quite a programme of entertainment.

A platform was put up in the library, with curtains to draw in front of it, and as this was done very easily and quickly, Patty rightly judged it had often been done before.

At last the time came, and everything was in readiness. The party was to begin at seven, and promptly at that hour the boys and girls began to arrive. Though seemingly so indifferent to every-day costumes, Cousin Elizabeth had taken much interest in dressing Patty and Ruth for this occasion, and Patty looked very sweet and pretty arrayed as Little Bo-Peep. Cousin Tom had chosen this character for her, and had helped to design the dress. It was, of course, the garb of a dainty little shepherdess, and it had blue panniers over a quilted white satin petticoat, and a black velvet bodice laced over a white chemisette.

Then Patty wore a broad brimmed hat trimmed with roses and fluttering ribbons. High-heeled slippers with bright buckles and a crook tied with blue ribbons added to the quaint effect, and the whole costume was very becoming to pretty Patty.

Ruth looked equally well, though in a very different way.

She represented the Puritan Maiden, Priscilla; who, though not a juvenile character was one of Ruth's favorite heroines, and the dress suited her so well, that Cousin Elizabeth said she should wear it.

A straight, scant gown of Quaker gray silk, a soft white mull kerchief folded across her breast, and a white muslin cap, transformed Ruth into a demure little Puritan maid.

Her small, pale face and quiet eyes suited the character, and the modest garb was very becoming.

Among the guests were represented, Red

Ridinghood, Cinderella, Little Boy Blue, Simple Simon, and many other well-known personages from Fairy Tales or Mother Goose's Melodies.

Then there were characters from more recent books, such as Little Women, Alice in Wonderland, Master Skylark and even Arabella and Araminta, who were dressed exactly alike.

Historical characters were there too; the Princess in the Tower chatted amiably with Joan of Arc, while Lady Jane Grey compared notes with Pocahontas.

Some of the children wore such nondescript costumes that it was difficult to guess whom they intended to represent.

After all had arrived the programme of entertainment was begun.

The motley crowd was seated in the library and soon the curtains in front of the platform were drawn apart revealing a table on which was a large gramophone.

Cousin Tom manipulated the instrument and the children heard orchestral music, plantation songs, comic speeches, and finally the exhibition-day exercises of a district school, which made them all laugh. After this, several of the guests were called on to recite or to sing, and as they had been notified beforehand, they were prepared for the occasion, and exerted their best elocutionary and vocal efforts.

As her contribution to the entertainment, Patty sang several of Robert Louis Stevenson's child-songs, which are set to such beautiful music, and Ruth recited a portion of "The Courtship of Miles Standish."

Then the curtains were drawn, and soon after the lights in the room were all turned out. Then the curtains flew open again disclosing a white sheet brightly illuminated from behind.

Somebody read aloud the poem by Richard Barham about "The Knight and the Lady," while a shadow pantomime representing the action of the ballad was shown on the sheet.

It was very funny.

Cousin Elizabeth was the Lady Jane, who was "tall and slim," while the part of Sir Thomas was wonderfully well acted by Cousin Tom, and when that portly old gentleman, who it seems was a naturalist, went around "unearthing his worms and his grubs," he looked very funny indeed.

And then when

> " Close by the side
> Of the bank he espied
> An uncommon fine tadpole, remarkably fat;
> He stooped, and he thought her his own, he had caught her,
> Got hold of her tail, and to land almost brought her,
> When, he plumped head and heels into fifteen feet water,"

and the shadow Sir Thomas ducked suddenly
into the pond, and a very real splashing was
heard, the delighted audience fairly shouted with
laughter.

And then when the funny old gardener appeared, bringing to the august Lady Jane the
news of Sir Thomas' fate, and when the jocund
Captain McBride tried to console the weeping
lady,—but, no, I can't tell it all to you; to see
how funny it all was you will have to read the
ballad in the " Ingoldsby Legends " for yourself.

When that was over, sandwiches, ices and
cakes were served and they seemed to be as
thoroughly enjoyed by the young people as were
Aunt Isabel's elaborate feasts, though by contrast it seemed to Patty a very slight repast.

Next came the " Quotation Salad " which was
Ruth's pride and delight.

Cousin Elizabeth passed around a great bowl,

which seemed to be full of leaves of crisp, green lettuce.

They were, however, made of tissue paper, and each leaf had attached to it a strip of writing paper on which was written a quotation.

These were from well-known poems or historic speeches, or even from Mother Goose's Melodies and other juvenile classics.

Each child drew out three leaves, and endeavored to remember or guess the source of the quotations written thereon.

Then the roll was called, and all who could give their three answers correctly were marked one hundred.

After this, the unguessed ones were read aloud, and whoever could answer them received ten more on his or her score for each perfect answer.

To the child attaining the highest score, a prize of a Dictionary of Quotations was to be awarded.

Patty's three questions were easy enough. One was " His cause is marching on."

Another was " Twinkle, twinkle little bat," and the third was " Don't give up the ship."

She could place all three, but when the more difficult ones were announced, she found that she knew very little about general literature.

Ruth, however, could tell the author of nearly every one, and no one was surprised when her score was declared the highest.

However, as she was the hostess, she declined to accept the prize, and it was given to the guest whose score stood the next highest.

Other intellectual or literary games were played, and at eleven o'clock the children were sent home, and Aunt Hester bade Ruth and Patty go to bed at once, lest they should not feel like getting up at the usual hour the next morning.

Patty heartily thanked Cousin Elizabeth for taking so much pains to make the party a pleasant one, and ran away to bed, wondering if many little girls had such clever relatives.

The spring flew by, and Patty could scarcely realize that she had been in Boston nearly three months, when a letter came from Mrs. Barlow, her mother's sister, at whose house she was to visit next.

" My dear Patty," her Aunt Grace wrote, " we

are going to our country home on Long Island
about the first of June, and we want you to come
to us as soon as we get settled there. No,—not
settled, we're never that, but as soon as we get
enough things straightened out to live with.
Our country-place is called ' The Hurly-Burly,'
so you may prepare yourself to see a family that
lives up to that name. But there is plenty of
amusement, if you are fond of boating and bathing, and we will all welcome you with open arms
and glad hearts; and the sooner you come, the
better we shall like it. Your cousins, Bob and
Bumble are very anxious to see you, and are
making wonderful plans for your entertainment.
So come as soon as you can, and if you will let
us know at what hour to expect you, Uncle
Theodore will meet you at the Grand Central
Station in New York, and bring you over to us
at Long Island.

" Your loving Aunt,

" GRACE BARLOW."

" But I don't want you to go," said Ruth,
when she heard the letter read; " I'd like to have
you stay here always."

Patty was surprised at this, for Ruth had always seemed so cold and unresponsive, that it didn't seem as if she had any affection in her nature.

The other members of the Fleming family echoed Ruth's sentiments, and though Patty felt sure their expressions were honestly meant, yet she thought, too, that as soon as she had gone, she would be forgotten in the rush of their busy life.

One morning in early June as they sat at the breakfast-table, Patty received a telegram, which said:

"Come at once before all are drowned. Grand Central five.

"HELEN BARLOW."

Although Patty didn't know it, Helen was the real name of her cousin who was always called Bumble, and Patty, horror-stricken at the import of this message, read it aloud, asking what it could mean.

The Fleming family were entirely unacquainted with the Barlows, and could give no clue, but one and all were filled with consternation at the peremptory summons.

Cousin Tom took the yellow paper and perused it carefully, then said :

"One thing is clear, at any rate, Patty, they expect you to be at the Grand Central Station in New York to-day at five o'clock, and you shall be there, for I'll take you myself."

So they all helped with the packing, and succeeded in getting one trunk ready for Patty to take with her, promising to send her other belongings after her a few days later.

With hurried good-byes and a promise of another visit to Boston at some future time, Patty went away with Cousin Tom, and they took the train for New York.

# CHAPTER XII

### THE HURLY-BURLY

PATTY and Cousin Tom reached the Grand Central station in New York about six o'clock, and leaving the train, went in search of any member of the Barlow family who might be there to meet them.

They hadn't walked a dozen steps before they were confronted by three broadly smiling faces.

These faces belonged to a tall, large man with his arms full of bundles, and a boy and girl who seemed both to be about Patty's own age.

"You're Patty, I know it,—I know it!" cried the girl, and she flung her arms round Patty's neck and kissed her heartily. "I am Bumble, and this is Bob, my twin; oh, I'm so glad to get you."

By this time Bob was shaking Patty's hand vigorously, and Mr. Barlow was trying to squeeze all of his bundles into one arm, that he might have a hand free to offer his niece.

134

Then Patty introduced Cousin Tom, and the party all went into the waiting-room together.

"But who sent me that telegram? and who is Helen?" inquired Patty, as she walked along with one of her twin cousins clinging to either arm.

"Oh, that's me," said Bumble. "My real name's Helen, but nobody ever calls me it."

"Because she's like a bumble-bee," explained Bob. "She's always tumbling about and knocking into people, and she's so buzzy and fat."

"Yes," said Bumble, good-naturedly, "I am; I'd like to be slim and graceful like you, but I'm not, so I just put up with myself and have all the fun I can."

Mr. Barlow gave Mr. Fleming a cordial invitation to continue his journey with Patty, and spend the night at "The Hurly-Burly," as his country-place on Long Island was called, but Cousin Tom declined, saying he had business in New York.

"But, Patty," he said, "your new-found relatives seem to be in no immediate danger of drowning."

"No," said Patty, who was consumed with

curiosity to know what the telegram could have meant.

"Drowning!" exclaimed Mr. Barlow, "what are you talking about? The bathing is very safe at our place; there's really no danger at all, unless one is positively foolhardy."

"No," said Patty, "but my telegram said ——"

"Oh, I know," broke in Bumble. "Papa left it to me to send you word to come to-day, and I didn't get at it until it was too late to write, so I telegraphed,—and I was so afraid you wouldn't get here before the kittens were drowned, that I mentioned it to make you hurry up."

"Kittens!" exclaimed Patty, laughing, "you didn't say kittens."

"I know it, but the ten words gave out too soon. I just had room to get in that we'd meet you at five o'clock. Oh, the kittens are such dears! Two black ones and a white one and a spotted one —— The white one is the prettiest, but she's an idiot, poor thing."

Cousin Tom was relieved to learn that no human beings were in jeopardy of their lives, but he secretly thought that Patty's new home was to be among very erratic people.

He bade his small cousin good-bye with real regret, for he and Patty had become firm friends during her Boston visit. After Mr. Fleming had left them, Mr. Barlow picked up all his bundles and packages, and telling the three children to follow him, he stalked away at a rapid pace.

Bob took Patty's satchel and Bumble took her umbrella, then they each grasped her arm and marched her along after their father.

" You see," explained Bob, " dad walks so very fast that we have to scurry to keep him in sight. So we'll boost you along,—it'll only be a minute."

And sure enough in a moment Mr. Barlow stopped at a street-car, and turned around expecting to find the children at his elbow, and there they were. He put them on the car, jumped on himself, and they all went over to the ferry.

A ride across the East River on the ferry-boat, and then a short ride in the cars brought them to the station of Sandy Cove.

Here Mr. Barlow expected his own carriage to be awaiting them, but no carriage was in sight. As it was growing dusk, and their home was still two miles distant, this was very annoying.

"I'll walk over home, and bring the carriage back for you," volunteered Bob; "it must be that Dil has forgotten to come for us."

"No," said his father, "you needn't do that,— we'll all jog along together and probably we'll meet Dil on the way."

"Dil is the man who takes care of our horse," said Bumble, as they walked along. "That's short for Dilatory, and we call him that 'cause he's so slow. In fact, we never know whether he's coming for us, or not."

And, apparently, this time Dilatory was not coming, for the travelers walked all the way without meeting the carriage. As they walked up the path, Patty was somewhat surprised to see that what Mr. Barlow called a cottage was in reality a large house. Wide verandas ran all the way round it on both the first and second stories, and magnificent trees waved their branches around and over it.

"This is the Hurly-Burly, Patty," said her uncle, "and if anything isn't quite in order, you must pardon it, for we're scarcely settled yet, and haven't had time to get everything to rights; and your Aunt Grace had the misfortune to sprain her ankle yesterday, so she can't attend to things as she otherwise would. But whatever you want just you come straight and tell your Uncle Teddy, and you shall have it, if it's a roc's egg."

Patty laughed, for she well knew what happened once when a roc's egg was asked for.

Then they entered the main front door, and Patty found herself in a wide hall that ran straight through the house with a door at either end.

There were large rooms on both sides of the hall, and following her uncle into one of these rooms, which was the sitting-room or general living-room of the family, Patty saw a remarkable sight. In a large armchair sat a sweet-faced lady, with an ottoman in front of her, on which her bandaged foot was resting on a pillow. She was reading a book, which she laid down as she heard people approaching, and over her head she held an open umbrella.

This was a wise precaution, for a drenching rain was pouring on the umbrella, and water dripped steadily from the ends of its ribs.

" Why, Grace," exclaimed Mr. Barlow, " what are you doing? What has happened? "

" The tank must have burst," returned his wife, placidly, " but fortunately I had this umbrella by me, so I opened it, and as you see, I am scarcely wet at all. Is this Patty? Come here, my dear. I am your Aunt Grace, your mother's sister, and I am prepared to love my little niece very much."

Patty returned very willingly her aunt's loving caress, and the two nestled together under the big umbrella, while Bob and Bumble laughed at the funny picture they made.

Uncle Ted had hastily dropped all his bundles on the hall table, and had run up-stairs to see what was the matter with the tank.

" I have a sprained ankle, Patty," said her aunt, by way of explanation of her predicament, " and I can't move a step. So I keep a cane near me to knock on the floor when I want anybody to fetch me things, but the cane got mislaid somehow, so I had this umbrella in its place. And wasn't it fortunate? For when the water began to drip down I just put up the umbrella and protected myself perfectly. The only trouble was, I couldn't close it to knock on the floor without getting myself drenched, so, as I had an interesting book I just waited patiently for somebody to come. The servants have gone on an excursion and Nan is away, too, so there was no one to knock for except old Dilatory, and he wouldn't have heard me anyway. Now, Bob, if you'll get another umbrella to hold over yourself while you move me to dryer quarters I'll be truly grateful."

" Take mine," said Patty, running to fetch it, and then she held her open umbrella over Bob while he wheeled his mother's chair across the hall and into the music-room.

Bumble moved the ottoman at the same time, and though she meant to be very careful, she bumped the wounded foot terribly when going over the door-sills, but Mrs. Barlow pretended it didn't hurt her, and thanked the children lovingly for their assistance. " Now, Bob," she said, " run and help your father. I suppose he's up in the tank-room investigating the source of that waterfall. Tell him he'd better send Dil for a plumber at once; and Bumble, you go and see if cook has returned yet, for if not, I don't know when we'll get any dinner. Patty, dear, take off your hat and jacket and then come and sit here by me, and we'll have a little talk. You remind me very much of your mother at your age. Do you remember her at all ? "

" No, Aunt Grace; I wish I could, but she died when I was only three, you know. I have a beautiful picture of her."

" Have you ? you must show it to me when your trunks come. You are like your mother in form and feature, and I hope your disposition is like hers. She was the loveliest woman I ever knew. So sweet and gentle, and so unselfish."

" I think you look like her picture, Aunt Grace," said Patty, gazing earnestly at her aunt.

" Oh, no, child; she was a hundred times more beautiful than I. And she was so neat and dainty, and always did the right thing at the right time. I was the harum-scarum of the family, and I'm sorry to say, my children seem to have inherited my traits of character. They are so careless, forgetful and unsystematic. But they're dear sweet children, and I hope, Patty, you will learn to love your Barlow cousins."

" I don't need to learn, Aunt Grace, I love

them already. Bob is such a frank, pleasant boy, and Bumble is a dear; so witty and bright."

"Yes, they are intelligent; and if you will be patient with our shortcomings, I think we will be very happy together. And our household, at present, contains another member. Nan Allen, who is visiting here, is a neighbor of ours in Philadelphia, and though several years older than you, she is a most charming young woman, and I'm sure you will like her. Gracious! how the water is pouring down in the sitting-room yet. I wish I could get up on my feet. Run up-stairs, Patty, and find your Uncle Ted, and ask him what is to be done about it?"

Although unacquainted with the house, Patty ran up-stairs, and through various rooms, but without finding her uncle.

Anxious to do her aunt's bidding, she ran on up to the third story, and in a large attic room she found her uncle standing before a large old-fashioned bookcase, eagerly reading a volume which he held in his hands.

"What about the water, Uncle Ted?" said Patty.

"Yes,—in a minute,—I'm going to attend to

it. I'm so surprised to find all these books here. We rented this cottage furnished, you know, and I haven't been up here before. I'd no idea these books were here. Yes,—I'll see about the water at once."

Patty went with her uncle to what he called the tank-room, and there Mr. Barlow discovered that the leak was in a supply pipe which could easily be shut off. This he did, and the downpour was immediately stopped, although no water could be drawn through the house until the plumbers should come and repair the pipes.

"Ted," said Mrs. Barlow, as her husband and Patty returned, "I don't believe Hopalong will be home in time to cook dinner, so suppose we have a pick-up supper? It's getting late, and Patty must be nearly starved after her journey from Boston."

"All right," said Uncle Ted, cheerily; "is there anything in the house to eat? Where's Bumble?"

"Go and hunt her up, please, and tell her I want her. And did you get the cheese and fruit as I asked you to?"

" Yes, I bought out the whole market and carried it all home with me."

" Very well, then we won't starve. Now wheel me into the dining-room and I'll see what we have on hand."

Just then Bob and Bumble appeared, each carrying two kittens, and these four sprawling bits of animal life were deposited in Mrs. Barlow's lap, while Patty was called upon to admire them.

" They are very cunning," said she, stroking them rather gingerly, for they seemed very small and frail.

" Oh, you can't hurt them," said Bob; " see, pick 'em up this way," and he grasped one by the back of its neck and held it sprawling in the air.

" No, hold one this way," said Bumble, cuddling a little ball of fur in the palm of her hand. " But, mumsey, I'm awful hungry; aren't we going to have any dinner? Where's Hopalong? "

" She's gone on the excursion, my dear. Poor thing, she works so hard I'm glad for her to have a little outing."

"H'm, she gets one about twice a week," said Bob; "Hopalong's the cook, Patty. We call her that 'cause she isn't very lively, and she just shuffles about. But she's a good-natured old thing, and such a good cook——"

"Here, children, take this flock of cats," said Mrs. Barlow, "and we'll soon have something to eat, cook or no cook."

Bumble gathered up the kittens, beginning with the white one. "This is the idiot," she said, "but isn't it a pretty cat? You can see she's half-witted, 'cause only one eye is open, and she has such a general air of stupidity."

"She might turn out to be the smartest of the lot," said Patty.

"I wish I could keep her and see, but dad says they must all be drowned to-morrow. I neglected the last kitten I had, and didn't feed her regularly, so the poor thing died. Daddy, if you'll let me keep this one, I'll never, *never* forget to feed her—honest I won't. Please let me keep just this one," and Bumble rubbed the furry ball on her father's cheek.

"Well, take them away now, and we'll see about it," said her father, and Bumble danced off with the kittens feeling almost sure that she had gained her point.

Then Bob and his father moved Mrs. Barlow with her chair and footstool out to the dining-room.

" I don't know what there is, myself," she said, " but we'll forage in the sideboard and pantry and see."

The foraging resulted in a pair of cold roasted ducks, plenty of plum-cake and a cherry-pie.

" I'm sorry there isn't any bread," said Mrs. Barlow, apologetically; " I told Hopalong to order it as she went by the baker's, but I fear she forgot it."

" Never mind," said Bob, " I don't care much for bread, anyhow, do you, Patty? Mother, here's a lot of cold potatoes. Can't you make a salad?"

" Yes, indeed," said Mrs. Barlow; so the children brought the ingredients, and a fine salad was soon concocted.

While this was going on, Miss Allen came running in.

" Oh," she exclaimed, " I'm as hungry as a hunter. We've been out sailing, and I've *such* an appetite. Who is this pretty child?"

" This is Patty Fairfield," said Bumble, " my cousin, from the South."

" Oh, yes, of course, I knew you expected her to-day. How do you do, Patty? I'm very glad to see you. I am Nan Allen, and I want you to like me better than you do any of the Barlows. Do you hear? "

" Yes," said Patty, " but I'll wait until I see if you like me."

Miss Allen was a very pretty young lady, of about twenty, with sparkling black eyes, and a lot of curly golden hair, which she wore massed high on her head. She was extremely vivacious and Patty liked her at once.

Then Bumble set the silver basket on the table, and Nan brought a pile of plates and everybody helped himself or herself to such viands as they wished.

There was much laughter and gay talk, and Patty enjoyed the informal meal immensely.

# CHAPTER XIII

## HOME-MADE MUSIC

"Why do you call this the music-room?" asked Patty; "there's no piano in it, nor any musical instrument that I can see."

"That's just the reason why," replied Nan. "I christened the room myself, and I called it the music-room because it hasn't anything musical in it. I get so tired of seeing music-rooms filled with pianos and banjos and mandolins and guitars. This is a refreshing change. And besides, when we want music we can sing."

"Then won't you sing now?" said Patty. "I'd like to hear you."

"Why, of course we will; would you like to hear some of our original songs?"

"Yes, indeed! Do you make songs yourself?"

"Oh, we always make our own songs. Home-made songs are ever so much better than boughten ones. They fit better and wear

149

longer.   We don't make the tunes, though ; we just appropriate those.   First we'll sing you ' The Song of the House.' "

This was sung to the air of " The Kerry Dance," and the whole family joined their voices with Nan's, and all sang with great spirit.

> Come, oh, come to the Hurly-Burly,
>     Come and join in the jolly fun
> That begins in the morning early,
>     And continues till day is done.
>
> Sailing, swimming, walking, riding,—
>     On the land or on the sea ;
> At the Hurly-Burly biding,
>     We're as happy as we can be.
>
> Oh, the jollity, oh, the gayety,
>     Just come down and see ;
>
> CHORUS :—Come, oh, come, etc.
>
> Sometimes we take sandwiches of chick,
> And go off on a merry pick-a-nick ;
> Sometimes we in hammocks idly swing,
> At other times we only sit and si-i-ng—
>
> CHORUS :—Come, oh, come, etc.

" That's beautiful," said Patty when they had finished the song.   " I'll learn the words, and then I can sing it with you."

" Indeed you must," said Nan, " and now I'll sing you the song of the Barlow family ; they won't sing it themselves, but when you learn it, you and I can warble it together."

> " Sing a song of Barlows,
>   A family full of fun ;
> A father and a mother,
>   A daughter and a son.
>
> " When the door is open
>   Hear the family sing !
> All the people passing by
>   Run like anything."

" It's a base libel," said Uncle Ted ; " we sing beautifully, and except that Bumble flats, and Bob has no ear, there isn't a flaw in our singing."

The evening passed merrily by, and when it was bedtime, Bumble showed Patty to her room.

When Patty found that a large front room on the second floor had been allotted to her, she expressed a fear lest she might be inconveniencing some one else by taking one of the choice rooms of the house.

" Not a bit," said Bumble. " Nan has the tower-room, because she likes it better, and the house is so big, there are plenty of rooms, anyway. Of course, if a lot of company comes, we may ask you to give up this, and take a smaller room, but you wouldn't mind that, would you?"

"No, indeed," said Patty. "I'll move out at any time." Then Bumble kissed her cousin good-night and went away.

Patty's trunk had been placed in her room, and she found that some one had kindly un-fastened its straps and clasps, so she had only to unlock it. She unpacked her clothes, and hung up her dresses in the wardrobe and cupboard, and put things neatly away in the bureau-drawers.

She placed her mother's picture on a small table, and looking at it critically, she concluded that it was like Aunt Grace, but much prettier.

After this, Patty looked round the great room with much interest. It seemed to contain a per-fect hodge-podge of furniture. There were three dressing-bureaus, and a huge wash-stand with two bowls and pitchers on it. There were sev-eral large easy-chairs, and an old haircloth sofa; there were small tables, and bookcases, and a cabinet filled with bric-a-brac, but,—and Patty could scarcely believe her eyes,—there was no bed!

When this fact dawned upon her, she con-cluded that one of the bookcases or bureaus must be a folding-bed.

She tried to open them, but the bureau-draw-ers and the bookcase-shelves proved themselves to be really what they seemed; then she looked for a bed concealed in an alcove or an ante-room, but the curtains hid only windows and the doors opened into ordinary closets.

Patty even looked in the fireplace and up the chimney, but she was gradually forced to the conclusion that there was no bed at her disposal, and that she must either report this fact to some member of the family or sit up all night.

As it was now late she hesitated to trouble anybody about the matter, and thought she would rather manage without a bed.

She did think of asking Bumble to let her share her room, but she didn't know where her cousin's room was, and too, there might be only a single bed in it. So Patty decided to try the old sofa.

As she had no pillow or bed-clothing, she rolled up a dress to put under her head and pinned two skirts together for a coverlet.

But the old haircloth scratched her bare feet, and poor Patty soon jumped up and sought another resting-place.

She cuddled up in a big armchair which was soft and warm, and there she soon fell asleep. But later, she awoke, so stiff from her cramped position, that she could scarcely move. So then she lay down on the floor and slept there the rest of the night.

Next morning she dressed herself and went down-stairs at about eight o'clock, but nobody was in sight, so Patty went out on the veranda and watched the waves as they came rolling and tumbling up on the beach.

Then, with a view to exploring her new home, she walked round the house.

This brought her to the kitchen, and through the window she saw a fat old black woman raking vigorously at the range.

"Dis yer stove 'll make me lose my 'ligion," Patty heard her murmur, and she felt sure she was listening to old Hopalong. "Good-morning, Hopalong," she cried.

"'Mawnin', missy; an' who be you?"

" I'm Patty Fairfield, and I'm Mrs. Barlow's niece, and I've come to stay all summer."

" Dat's good. I see you'se a nice, pretty-behaved little lady. Any ob de fam'ly 'round yit?"

" No, I haven't seen anybody."

" Well, yere comes Massa Ted; now I mus' jes' be spry 'bout gettin' my co'n brade done."

Hopalong shuffled away, and Patty turned to see Uncle Ted coming towards her.

" Hello, Patty-girl," he cried, " you're up betimes."

" Yes," said Patty, " and so are you. Oh, Uncle Teddy, isn't the sea gorgeous? I do love it so, and I'm so glad I'm here ! "

" That's good, little one ; I'm glad you're glad. And now come to breakfast."

Aunt Grace had been carried down-stairs by her husband and son, and was already in her place at the table.

She called Patty to her and kissed her affectionately, and asked her if she slept well. Patty hesitated a moment, then breaking into a merry laugh, she said:

" Why, Auntie Grace, I *didn't* sleep very well, for I hadn't any bed."

"What?" exclaimed her aunt, in horror, "why, Patty, I ordered a little brass bed sent from Philadelphia purposely for you, and it arrived yesterday morning. I told Dil to put it up in your room, and I told Eunice to see that it was properly made. But I confess I did forget to ask if my orders had been carried out, and,— I suppose they weren't. You poor child! How did you manage? Why didn't you tell us?"

"Well, I didn't notice it until quite late," said Patty. "I was so busy putting my clothes and things away, that I never thought of anything else at the time. And, anyway, I didn't mind for one night."

Just then Bumble came in, and when she heard about Patty's experience she looked astounded. "Why," said she, "I took Patty to her room myself, and I never noticed that there was no bed there!"

"You're a rattle-pated goosey," said her father; "but never mind, Patty, you shall have two beds to-night to make up for it,—I'll promise you that."

"Don't believe him," cried Nan, gayly, as she ran into the dining-room. "I don't know what

Uncle Ted is saying to you,—but he won't do it. He never kept a promise in his life!"

"'Oh, promise me,'" began Uncle Ted, and then they all joined in and sang:

"Oh, promise me that some day you and I
   Will take a piece of huckleberry pie,
   Some deviled eggs and strawberry ice cream,
   And have a picnic down by yonder stream.
   And then we'll wander through the fields afar,
   And take a ride upon a trolley car;
   But we'll come home again in time for tea,—
   Oh, promise me—oh, promise me-e-e—"

The last refrain rang out with a prolonged wail that seemed to Patty the funniest thing she had ever heard, and she fairly shouted with laughter.

"Oh, dear, you are the funniest family," she exclaimed; "I think I shall stay here six months instead of three."

# CHAPTER XIV

## A FUNNY FAMILY

PATTY was right when she called the Barlows a funny family, for their spirits were irrepressible, and each day, from morning till night was filled with jokes and absurdities accompanied or followed by gales of laughter.

But they were heedless, forgetful people, and the whole household showed an utter lack of systematic management.

Nothing was ever to be found in its place; meals were served at any hour when old Hopalong got them ready. Sometimes the market orders were neglected and there was almost nothing to eat, and then again there was such an overstock that much had to be wasted. The children were allowed to do exactly as they chose, and were never reproved; but if their own mischief led them into misfortune, or their pranks turned out disastrously, they were expected to stand the consequences bravely, and look for little or no sympathy from their elders.

Patty had not been at the Hurly-Burly many days before she discovered that its proportion of order and regularity was entirely too small. To be sure, in the Fleming family it had been too large; but she thought there must be a happy medium, a state of things whereby one could expect the ordinary events of daily life to come in due course, without, however, living as if by clockwork. You see Patty was becoming a very wise little girl, for she was profiting by her varied experiences, and trying to learn the best way to take care of her father's house and make it a real home for him. Sometimes she felt this responsibility very greatly, and longed for some motherly, housewifely friend to talk with about it.

But Aunt Grace, though loving and affectionate, was no help in such matters.

"Nonsense, child," she would say, "don't worry about your housekeeping; why, the house will keep itself, if you let it alone. And you're too young to be bothered with a weight of domestic care, anyway. Now run off and play with Bob and Bumble. Go for a row or a drive and let the breeze blow all such worries out of your little noddle."

So Patty ran away and played with her cousins, and they did have jolly good times.

There were so many nice things to do; fishing, sailing, bathing, boating, driving, golf, tennis, and all sorts of outdoor amusements were at their disposal.

The Barlow twins, Nan Allen and Patty made a gay quartette, and if they desired a larger party, there were plenty of neighbors ready to join in their fun.

One warm afternoon, Patty and Bumble sat in a hammock swung under the trees, while Bob sprawled on the grass near them.

"Girls," said he, "come on, let's go for a swim. The Smiths and the Enfields just went down towards the bath-houses, and there'll be a jolly crowd in the water."

"All right, let's go," replied his sister. "Where's Nan?"

"She's in the house somewhere," said Patty. "I'll go find her."

Patty ran into the house and looked in at the music-room door, as a beginning of her search, but there she saw such a startling sight that she stood spellbound, unable to go any further.

At the writing-desk sat a person whose head was entirely bald. Not a spear of hair was anywhere visible on the bare, pinky-white scalp, and the round head was smooth and shiny as a billiard-ball.

Then the head turned round and faced Patty, with rolling eyes and a weird grimace. But Patty looked so astounded and frightened that the face broke into a reassuring smile, and Nan's voice said:

"Why, Patty, don't be scared; it's only I. Didn't you know I wore a wig? There it is, on that chair."

And sure enough, there was Nan's mop of frizzed, flaxen hair hanging on a chair-back.

"But," said Patty, coming nearer, and still unable quite to comprehend it all, "why don't you have any hair yourself?"

"Well, you see," said Nan, as she sealed and addressed the letter she had been writing, "I had typhoid fever just before I left home, and my hair came out so, that I had to have it all shaved off. So now I am wearing a wig until it grows again. But it is so warm to-day, I took my wig off for a few moments to rest my head."

Patty examined the wig with great interest.

" I think it's wonderful," she said, " is it just like your own hair was ? "

" No, indeed, I wanted a change.  My own hair is very dark, almost black, and perfectly straight.  So I bought this Flaxie Frizzle wig for a change.  It's becoming, don't you think so ?  I have a red wig too,—of short, curly auburn hair.  Sometimes I wear that."

Patty watched Nan curiously, as she put the wig on, securing it to her head by invisible springs.

" I never saw anybody with a wig before," she said, " and it surprises me so ; but I came to ask you to go swimming with us."

" Can't do it," said Nan ; " I have two more letters to write, and then I'm going driving with the Perrys.  They're to call for me at four o'clock, and it's after three now.  You'll have to go without me this time."

" All right," said Patty, backing out of the room, for her eyes were still fixed on the wonderful wig.

Then she rejoined her cousins, and they all ran down to the bath-houses.

They had a fine bath, and were about ready to come out of the water when Nan appeared.

She was dressed in a fresh white piqué suit, with blue ribbons at her throat and belt, and was looking very pretty but decidedly disappointed.

She walked out to the end of the narrow wooden pier, and the swimmers came up to talk to her.

Patty didn't swim very well as yet, but she was learning, and Uncle Ted and Bob said she was getting along finely.

" I thought you were going out with the Perrys," cried Bumble.

" I was, —" said Nan, "but they didn't come. I've been dressed and waiting for them half an hour, then I looked again at the note they sent me, and I made a mistake; it's to-morrow they asked me to go. So I came down here, and I wish I was in the water with you."

" Come on in," said Bob.

" Too much trouble to get into my bathing-suit."

" Don't do it," said Bumble; " we're coming out now, anyway. But the water is fine, to-day, isn't it, Patty?"

"Glorious!" gurgled Patty, as she floundered about in her frantic endeavors to swim. Suddenly, Nan snatched off her wig, and dropped it down on the dock.

Then with dramatic gestures, she wrung her hands, waved them above her head, and cried out in agonized tones:

"I am desperate! No longer can I bear this sad and weary life. I *will* end it!" Apparently in the last stages of despair, she strode to the end of the dock, and threw herself headlong into the water.

Patty was aghast, but Bob and Bumble were accustomed to Nan's mad tricks, and they shouted with laughter.

In a moment the bald head reappeared above the water, for Nan could dive and swim wonderfully well.

"I'm afraid my dress will get wet," she said, "but when I saw you all having such fun, I just couldn't help jumping in."

"Crazy Nan," said Bumble, "you've spoiled your clean dress, and you can't swim with your shoes on, anyway, can you?"

"Not very well," said Nan, regretfully, and

they're my best shoes, too.  But I don't care; I'll get a bath and have some fun."

Later on, the four young people, much refreshed and exhilarated, assembled in the music-room to wait for dinner.

Aunt Grace, whose sprained ankle was getting better, and who could now limp around with the aid of a crutch, was there too.

"Geranium Blossom! but I'm hungry," exclaimed Bob.  "Mumsey, do you s'pose we're going to have any dinner to-night?"

"I think so, my boy," returned Mrs. Barlow, placidly, "but go and get a biscuit if you'd like one."

"I'll tell you what," said Nan, "let's have tea while we wait.  There'll be plenty of time, for Eunice has just begun to lay the table for dinner."

"All right," said Bumble.  "Patty, if you'll get the hot water, I'll cut up a lemon."

"But there aren't any lemons," said her mother.  "I looked for one to-day, and they're all out."

"There aren't any biscuits, either," said Bob, coming back from a fruitless quest; "the box is empty."

" And there doesn't seem to be any sugar," said Nan, peering into the sugar-bowl on the tea-table.

" Well, I'll tell you what," said Bumble, " let's pretend to have tea. You know some people say, if you think you have anything, you have it."

" All right," said Patty, who dearly loved to pretend, " I'll make the tea."

So she pretended to measure out some tea from the caddy, and put it in the teapot. Then she poured imaginary water from the teakettle upon it, and covered the teapot tightly with the cosey. After allowing it a little time to " draw," she pretended to pour it into cups, in which Bumble had already placed imaginary sugarlumps and bits of lemon.

Bob offered his services as waiter, and passed the cups to his mother and Nan, and also to imaginary guests, who, he pretended, were sitting on the chairs and sofa.

" This tea is delicious," said Aunt Grace, stirring in her empty cup, and sipping from her empty spoon.

" Yes," said Patty, " it is real Russian tea. Do have some more, won't you ? "

"Indeed, I will," said Aunt Grace, and Patty poured her another empty cupful.

"Pass the biscuit, Bumble," said Bob, and his sister carried around the empty biscuit-jar, while the guests helped themselves to nothing.

Uncle Ted came in in the midst of the tea joke, and drank several cups of air, until Patty finally peeped into the teapot, and said, "You'll all have to stop, for there isn't any tea left."

Bob carried the cups back to the tea-table, and all declared they had had a very nice tea-party.

"But why don't you have a tea-party, girls?" said Uncle Ted, "a real one, I mean. Invite all the neighbors and have a nice spread. I'll decorate a bit with Japanese lanterns, and we'll make it a general festivity."

"Oh, lovely!" cried Bumble, "if mamma is well enough to stand the excitement."

"Aunt Grace needn't have any of the trouble," said Nan. "I'll order things, and help get the house ready. We girls will do all the work, and Aunt Grace can just be an invited guest."

"Let's make it a lawn-party," said Bob, "and we'll have supper served in a tent."

"Let me see," said Uncle Ted, "to-day is Monday. There's no use waiting too long, and the moon is nearly at its full now. Suppose we have the party on Thursday; can you all be ready by that time?"

"Oh, yes," said Nan, "there's nothing much to do. Let's write the invitations to-night."

So during dinner, which was finally announced, they completed their plans for a garden-party from five o'clock to ten Thursday evening; and after dinner Nan wrote the invitations, and Patty addressed them, while the rest discussed and decided who should be invited to the party.

# CHAPTER XV

## THE LAWN-PARTY

THE next day Patty announced her willingness to do anything she could to assist in the preparations for the lawn-party; and Aunt Grace kissed her fondly, and said she was a dear little helper, and they would be only too glad to make use of her services.

But the day passed by and nothing was done. Everybody went for a swim in the morning, and in the afternoon Nan went driving, and Patty and the twins were invited to a neighbor's to play tennis. Then in the evening they all went for a moonlight sail.

After they returned, Patty ventured to remind her procrastinating relatives that there was very little time left in which to prepare for the various entertainments they had suggested.

" Jumping grasshoppers ! " exclaimed Bob, whose expletives were often of his own invention, " I meant to set old Dil at work to-day,

169

clearing a place for a tent. Dad, we must go over to the city to-morrow, and get a tent, and some lanterns and flags. We want to make the place look gay and festive."

" Yes, we'll go," said his father, heartily, " and the girls can go with us, if they like."

" We *do* like," cried Bumble, " and after we buy the things, won't you take us to the Zoo, to see the baby hippopotamus ? "

" But," said Patty, " I think we ought to stay at home and help Aunt Grace."

" No, no," said her aunt, " there's nothing much to do ; I'll get somebody in to help Hopalong make cakes and jellies, and we can leave the house decorations until Thursday."

" Yes, that will be best," said Nan, " for to-morrow I'm going over to Montauk Point for the day, but I'll help all day Thursday."

" We'll all work with more enthusiasm when the day of the party comes," said Aunt Grace, " and now run along to bed, all of you."

Next day the family rose late, and breakfast was much later, so that it was noon before they started for New York.

Then Bob proposed that they go to the Zoo

first, and do the shopping afterwards. This they did, and the result was, that, as the animals were so interesting, after they had seen them all it was too late to go to the shops.

" Whew! I'd no idea it was so late," said Uncle Ted, looking at his watch; " but never mind. We'll go home now, and I'll telegraph early in the morning, and the tent and lanterns can be sent over at once, and we can easily get them put up in time."

When they reached home they found Aunt Grace entertaining some friends who had come to spend the day. They were delightful people, and Aunt Grace had found them so absorbing that she had entirely forgotten to send for an assistant to prepare dainties for the party.

But nobody seemed to mind, and Patty concluded it was not her place to comment on the way things were going, at least, not to the Hurly-Burly people themselves.

But when she wrote that night to her father, she said :

" I'm glad you didn't describe my aunts to me, but let me discover their traits for myself. For, really, I never would have believed a family

*could* act like the Barlows.    They are out of proportion *every* way, but, after all, I can't help loving them, for they are such dear, kind people,
and they *mean* to do right, only they never do
anything."

But as the next day was Thursday, and some
things *had* to be done, everybody began to hus-
tle and bustle and fly around generally.

Uncle Ted sent to New York by a special
messenger for a tent, and a lot of lanterns and
gay bunting, and succeeded in getting them soon
after noon.    Then he and Bob and old Dil put
the tent up, and hung the lanterns along the
veranda and among the trees.

Nan drove all around the country trying to
find a cook to assist Hopalong, but as none was
to be found, Aunt Grace had to go down to the
kitchen and make some of the cakes herself.

Nan and Bumble made sandwiches and
squeezed lemons, and somehow the time slipped
away until it was four o'clock, and the house was
not yet decorated and the ice cream hadn't arrived from New York.    " Nan, you and Patty
fix the flowers, and I'll take the trap and fly
down to the station and see if the ice cream

isn't there," said Bumble, who was very warm and tired, but who kindly offered to do the most unpleasant errand.

" All right," said Nan, and Bumble drove off in a hurry. That morning the girls had gathered a quantity of wild flowers and vines for decorations, and Bumble said she had put them in water, but nobody knew where. So they hunted in every place they could think of, but to no avail. Bob helped them and they searched the kitchen, the cellar, and even the barn, but no flowers could they find. So, as it was nearly five o'clock they gave it up and ran up-stairs to dress for the party.

And then Patty discovered that the bath tub was filled with the missing flowers. At risk of being caught by the guests in their every-day attire, Nan and Patty flew down-stairs and hastily arranged the flowers as well as they could, and then returned to make their toilettes.

It was now after five, but fortunately no guests had yet arrived.

" Nobody will come before half-past five, anyway," said Nan, as they hastily scrambled into their frocks.

"They may," replied Patty, "there comes somebody now; oh, it's Bumble."

Bumble came in, panting and breathless.

"I had to bring the ice cream home with me," she said; "there was no one else to bring it from the station. Wasn't it lucky I went over?"

"Yes, indeed," said Patty, "and now, Bumble dear, rest yourself a little. Nan and I will receive the guests. Aunt Grace is still in the kitchen."

"Yes," said Bumble, "but the table isn't set yet. We ought to get out the plates and things. Eunice is frosting cakes, and she can't do it."

"Well, I can do it now," said Patty. "I'm all ready, if you'll just tie my sash. Nobody is here yet, so I may have a few minutes at least."

But when Patty reached the dining-room the scene was appalling. In the hurry, nobody had found time to clear away the luncheon dishes, and the extension table must be made longer, and really there was an hour's work there for somebody.

Patty called Bob to help her, as everybody else was so busy, and the good-natured boy left what he was doing and came to his cousin's assistance.

It was six o'clock before everything was in readiness and the family gathered on the veranda to rest themselves and await their guests.

"Seems to me they're getting pretty fashionable," said Bob; "it's an hour after the time set, and nobody's here yet."

"Well, it's a warm day," said Aunt Grace, fanning herself, "and nobody likes to start out early in the afternoon." But after another half-hour passed and still nobody came, they all began to think it rather queer.

"Perhaps they've boycotted us," said Uncle Ted, "and don't mean to come at all."

"I should think the Perrys would be here by this time," said Nan. "I meant to speak to them about it yesterday, and ask them to be sure to come early, but I forgot it."

"Did we invite the Harlands?" said Bob.

"I can't think whether we did or not," said Bumble. "I know we were undecided about them. But we asked the Graysons, and here they come now."

"Well, I'm glad somebody's coming," said

Nan; " but, no,—they aren't turning in, they're driving by ! "

" Sure enough," said Bob; " mean old things, —if they couldn't come, they might at least have sent regrets."

" Here are the Stanton girls, anyway," said Patty, as two young ladies came walking towards them.

Elsie and Mildred Stanton came up to the group on the veranda with a slightly embarrassed air.

" Good-evening," said Mildred; " you look as if you were going to have a lawn-party."

" Why, we are," said Bumble, " if anybody comes to it. I'm glad you've arrived, anyway. Come in."

" But,—we weren't invited," said Elsie, a little stiffly. " We came over on an errand."

" Indeed you were invited," said Bumble, warmly. " Do you suppose I'd leave you out, my dearest chums ? But really, didn't you get an invitation ? How funny ! They were sent out on Tuesday."

" No," said Elsie, " but if it was a mistake, and you meant to invite us, it's all right. But we didn't know it, you see, so we're not in party frocks. As nobody else is here yet, I think we'll run home and dress up a bit, and then come back again."

"All right," said Bumble, knowing her guests would feel more comfortable if suitably dressed, —and they lived near by. "Skip along, girls, and hurry back."

After they had gone it was nearly seven o'clock, and nobody else appeared. Great consternation was felt by all, and suddenly Patty said, "Who mailed those invitations?"

"Bumble did," said Bob.

"No, I didn't," said Bumble, "I thought you attended to it. Why, Bob, I asked you particularly to look after them."

"I didn't hear you," said Bob; "do you suppose——"

But Patty had already run into the house and returned with her hands full of the invitations to the party.

"Oh," groaned everybody, quite overcome by the calamity.

Nan was the first to recover herself.

"There's only one thing to do," she said; "we

must go around and pick up as many guests as we can in a hurry. It won't do to let all this nice garden-party go to waste. Bob and I will také the runabout, and Bumble, you and Patty can take the trap, and we'll scour the country as far as possible."

In a few minutes the two turnouts dashed away in opposite directions, and all the near-by neighbors were bidden to come to the garden-party at once.

Much laughter and fun was caused by the sudden and peremptory invitations, which were, for the most part, gladly accepted.

When the guests finally arrived, the party was a grand success, though of much smaller proportions than was originally intended. The gayly-lighted veranda was a fine place for dancing and games, and supper, served in the tent, was very novel and attractive.

As Nan said, after the party was over, " It was just perfect, except that we couldn't invite the ones that lived at any distance."

But Uncle Ted said, " Never mind, we'll have another party, and invite them; and I'll see to mailing the invitations myself."

"Oh, ho," laughed Nan, "then we needn't even get ready for the party, for you'll never remember to post them."

At which Uncle Ted called her a saucy minx, and sent them all to bed.

# CHAPTER XVI

## UNBOUNDED HOSPITALITY

ALTHOUGH life at the Hurly-Burly was full of irritating incidents and even serious disappointments which were caused by the general forgetfulness and careless habits of the family, yet there were also many pleasures, and Patty enjoyed the summer very much and became warmly attached to her happy-go-lucky relatives.

Uncle Ted was kindness itself, and Aunt Grace was very loving and affectionate towards her motherless niece. Bob and Bumble were trumps, and Nan was so irresistibly funny that she made merry jokes of what would otherwise have been real troubles.

The days flew by and Patty thought she had never known a summer to pass so rapidly.

She almost lived out of doors, for Uncle Ted said he was determined to transform the little Boston bluestocking into a wild Indian; and so Patty had become browned by the sun, and her rowing and swimming had developed a fine amount of muscle.   But as we are always more or less influenced by the character of those about us, Patty had also imbibed much of the spirit of the  Hurly-Burly  family  and  lived  as  if  the pleasure of the present moment were the only thing to be considered.

"Be  careful,  my  Patty,"  her  father  wrote  to her, "you do not send me letters as regularly as you used to, and what you tell me sometimes sounds as if you thought it no harm to break a promise or to fail to keep an engagement you have made.   You know I want you to *learn* by  your experiences, and imitate only the best qualities of those about you.   I'm not going  to  have  my  house  run  on  any  Hurly-Burly  plan, Miss Pattikins, so if you expect to secure the position of housekeeper, you must be prepared  to  keep  things  right  up  to  the mark. We will have an exact proportion of methodical regularity, without having so much of it that it will be a bugbear.   Oh, I tell you, my lady, our  home  is  going  to  be  a  veritable  Paradise on earth, and I am impatient to get it started. You have only one more visit to make, and then

I will come and kidnap my own daughter and carry her off with me for a Christmas present."

"What a dear, wise father I've got," mused Patty, after reading this letter, "and how he understands everything, even without my telling him. I *will* try not to grow heedless and rattle-pated, though it's hard to be any other way in this house."

One morning in August, Mrs. Barlow said to her husband, "Ted, you know the Carletons are coming this afternoon to stay several days, and I want you to go over to the three o'clock train to meet them. Don't forget it, will you? And you'll have to engage a stage to bring them over, for there'll be Mr. and Mrs. Carleton and four children, and perhaps a nurse. I don't know where we're going to put them all to sleep, but we must stow them away somehow. Patty, would you mind giving up your room for a time?"

"Not a bit, Aunt Grace. Put me wherever you like."

"That's a good girl. Well, suppose you sleep with Bumble. She has only a three-quarter bed, but if you don't quarrel you won't fall out."

" All right," said Patty.  " I'll move my things at once."

" Very well, my dear; then we can give your room to Mr. and Mrs. Carleton, and Gertrude will have to room with Nan, and the other children must go up in the third story; no,—Harry can sleep with Bob. I declare I didn't think it would crowd us so, when I invited the whole family. But it will be only for a week, and we'll get along somehow."

" Many hands make light work," and with much flurrying and scurrying the rooms were made ready for the expected guests.

About noon the expressman came, bringing two trunks.

" ' Coming events cast their shadows before,' " said Uncle Ted; " here come the wardrobes of the Carleton family."

" They must have sent them by express yesterday," said Aunt Grace; " dear me, how forehanded some people are. I wish I had been born that way. But when I go anywhere I take my trunk with me, and then I always leave it behind."

They all laughed at this paradoxical statement,

and Uncle Ted said, " That's where you differ from an elephant." Then as the trunks were set out on the veranda, he exclaimed, " Good gracious, my dear, these aren't the Carleton's trunks. They're marked ' F. M. T.,'—both of them."

" ' F. M. T.,' " echoed Mrs. Barlow, " why, who can that be ? "

" The Carletons have borrowed other people's trunks to come with," suggested Nan.

" Not they," returned Aunt Grace; " they're the most particular people on the face of the earth. Why Kate Carleton would as soon think of borrowing a house as a trunk. No, these belong to somebody else. And I know who it is ! It's Fanny Todd. Before I left home I asked her to come down here the first week in August, and I never thought of it again from that day to this. But I should think she would have written."

" Why, mamma," said Bumble, " there was a letter came for you from Philadelphia a day or two ago. Didn't you get it? I saw it on the hall table."

" No, I didn't get it. Run and look for it, child."

But the letter couldn't be found. So Mrs.
Barlow assumed that it was from her friend, Miss
Todd, and concluded that that lady would shortly
arrive.

" Where *can* we put her to sleep?" she
queried, " every room is already filled."

" She can have my room," said Bob, " and
Harry Carleton and I will sleep out in the tent.
He's a good fellow and he won't mind."

" But his mother will," said Mrs. Barlow;
" she's so fussy about such things. Still, I can't
see anything else to do. If it doesn't rain, I suppose you'll be all right."

The Carletons came first, and Mrs. Barlow
welcomed them with a gracious hospitality which
gave no hint of the flurried turmoil of prepara-
tion that had been going on all day.

Gertrude Carleton, the eldest daughter, was
one of those spick-and-span beings who look as
if they ought always to be kept in a bandbox.
She had a languishing die-away sort of air, and
after a few moments' conversation with her,
Bumble excused herself and slyly nudged Patty
to come outside with her. She took her cousin
up-stairs and said, " Patsy, I'm sure that blown-

glass girl won't like to room with Nan. She looks as if she always had a whole suite of rooms to herself, parlor and all. I can imagine her fainting away when Nan takes off her wig. Now, how would it do to give Miss Gertrude our room, and you and I go in with Nan? I'll bunk on the sofa; I don't mind a bit."

"Neither do I," declared Patty. "Yes, let's give your room to the Lady Gertrude, and never mind asking Nan about it, either."

So the girls changed things around in short order, and then went down-stairs and conducted Gertrude to her room.

Aunt Grace gave a little surprised smile, but with her usual tact, said nothing.

Harry Carleton seemed to be a very nice boy, and he went off to the tent with Bob, in great glee, while the two little Carleton children and their nurse were installed in rooms on the third floor.

Before the guests had reappeared down-stairs, a carriage drove up to the veranda, and a lady and gentleman got out.

"Oh," thought Mrs. Barlow, as she went to greet them, "who *has* Fanny brought with her?"

"How do you do, Grace?" cried sprightly Miss Todd, "I've come, you see, though I didn't get the telegram I asked you to send me. And I brought Mr. Harris, as I said I would. I know you'll welcome him gladly after what I told you."

"Fanny," said Mrs. Barlow, deeming it best to make a clean breast of the matter, "I didn't get your letter. At least, they say it came, but somehow it was lost before I read it, and it can't be found. However, it doesn't matter, and I am very glad to welcome Mr. Harris in any capacity."

"Then greet me as Miss Todd's future husband," said Mr. Harris, smiling, and Mrs. Barlow gave him a hearty welcome and congratulations at the same time.

But Mr. Harris was a new problem. Although he intended to remain only one night, yet a room must be provided for him, and poor Mrs. Barlow was at her wits' end.

But it was at her wits' end that the good lady oftenest found a way out of her difficulties, and after a glance into Mr. Harris' merry blue eyes, she felt sure she could ask him to sleep on the couch in the music-room without offending his dignity in the least. And so it turned out that the Hurly-Burly was filled with guests, and it goes without saying that they all had a merry time.

Uncle Ted was in his element, and he provided fun for the children and entertainment for the older guests, until even languid Gertrude was stirred to enthusiasm.

It was late when they all retired, and after Mrs. Barlow had insured the comfort of her guests and her children, she lay down to rest and fell asleep at once.

# CHAPTER XVII

### A HURLY-BURLY FIRE

ALTHOUGH Mr. Harris had expressed himself satisfied with his couch in the music-room, yet as it was hard and narrow, his slumbers were not very profound, and at two o'clock in the morning he awoke from a light doze, and began to sniff in the darkness.

" I believe I smell fire," he said to himself.

He jumped up and ran into the hall, where he found the whole staircase was a charred and smouldering mass ready to break into flame at any moment.

Mr. Harris was a man of quick action, but he paused a moment to consider.

He couldn't go up the stairs, they were ready to give way at a touch. He dared not open the front door, or, indeed, any door that might create a draught which would fan the stairs into a flame.

So he decided he must rouse the sleepers up-stairs, and then jump out of the music-room window and run to the tent to get the assistance of the two boys who were sleeping there.

Being a stranger in the house, he knew of no other stairway, and knew nothing of the servants or where they might be.

" Mr. Barlow,—fire! Mr. Barlow!" he screamed. " Fire! Mr. Carleton, Fanny!" but no one answered.

At last Patty was wakened by his voice and ran out in the upper hall. The draught of her opening door started the flames a little, and when she looked over the banister, it was into a well of fire.

Before she could say a word, Mr. Harris called up to her. " Patty," he said, " keep your senses, and help all you can. I think the fire is only in the staircase, and if so, we can get everybody safely out of their own windows. Tell this to your uncle, and then tell the others. I'm going after Bob."

Mr. Harris disappeared, and Patty bravely resisted her inclination to scream ; instead, she ran into her uncle's room and shook him awake, saying, " Uncle Ted, the stairs are all burnt up ; but it doesn't matter, you can get out of the windows."

Then she ran back and wakened Bumble and Nan, saying, " Girls, the house is on fire, but let's be real sensible and not get burned up. Put on your dressing-gowns, and then we must go and tell the others."

As she talked Patty was slipping on her dressing-gown, and then she caught up her mother's picture and wrapped it in a bath-towel, and with the little bundle in her hand she ran back to the hall where she met Uncle Ted.

" Which room are the Carletons in, Patty ? " She told him, and then Bob shouted up from below, " We've got the old Babcock extinguisher, dad, and we're making it tell on the fire. Can't you throw on some water up there ? And tell all the people to go out on the balconies and we'll take 'em down all right. And I say, Patty, get my camera out of my room, will you? I don't want anything to happen to that."

" All right," said Patty, and she ran for the camera. In Bob's room she found Miss Todd just waking up.

" Get up, Miss Todd," she cried ; " the house

is on fire and your Mr. Harris is putting it out,
and he says for you to jump out of the window."

" Oh," screamed Miss Fanny, hopping out of
bed and rushing wildly around the room, " which
window ? "

" Any window," said Patty, who was hunting
in the closet for the camera.

So Miss Todd, half unconscious of what she
was doing, but with a blind intention of obeying
the orders of her fiancé, climbed over a window
sill and jumped out.

As  a veranda ran all  around the second-story
of the Hurly-Burly, she found herself standing
just  outside her window on a very substantial balcony and feeling decidedly chilly in the night air.

" Here are some clothes," said Patty, grabbing
up whatever came handy, and  putting them out
the window to Miss Todd.   " Is there anything
you want saved particularly ? "

For Patty had  taken a pillow-case from its
pillow, and in it had placed the bundle containing her mother's picture, and Bob's camera.

" Yes," said  Miss  Todd ;  " that  book  of
poems,—it was Jim's first gift to me.—oh, and
my hat."

" All right," said Patty, and she put the book in her pillow-case bag, but the hat, being large and feathery she put on her head.

Then Patty went to Gertrude Carleton's room. She found that fragile bit of humanity sleeping peacefully, and she hated to startle her.

But the excitement was growing greater. People were running about in all directions, and the flames, though still confined to the staircase, were liable to spread further at any moment. So Patty decided to break the news gently to the frail Gertrude, and she touched her softly on the shoulder.

" Gertrude, dear," she said, " if the house *should* get on fire, what would you want to save most ? "

" My shoes," said Gertrude, promptly, awake and alert in an instant. " Here they are."

She reached over the side of the bed, and grasped her dainty little patent-leather boots, which she gave to Patty.

" Very well," said Patty, putting them in her bag, " and now you'd better get up and dress, for the house may get on fire to-night. Come, I'll help you, for I smell smoke now."

"Where are you going with your hat on?" asked Gertrude, much bewildered, but still making an expeditious toilette.

"Nowhere," said Patty. "I'm collecting valuables; this is Miss Todd's hat. I must go now. When you're ready, step out of your window on to the balcony, and they'll take you down by ladders or something, I guess."

Patty went out into the hall, and found that the fire was partly under control. Uncle Ted and Mr. Carleton were pouring buckets of water on it, which they brought from the bathroom where Bumble was helping fill the buckets.

Down-stairs, Mr. Harris and the two boys were using hand grenades, an old fire extinguisher, and sundry other patented means of putting out fires. There was much yelling of orders going on, but very little obeying of the same, and each man seemed to be working with a will in his own way.

Patty went into her Aunt Grace's room, and found that lady dressed in her best attire.

"I thought I'd put on this gown," she said. "Ted says we'll all be saved; but then you never can tell how a fire may break out somewhere else

and burn up all your wardrobe. So I'll have
this, anyway, and it's my best gown. Ted told
me to stay in this room and not move until he
came after me. Is the fire burning the hall carpet much?"

"Yes, quite a good deal; but they've spilled
so much water on it that it's all wet, and I reckon
that will spoil it more than the fire. But, Aunt
Grace, what do you want to save? The house
may all burn up, you know, and I'm trying to
save the most valuable things. I've this pillow-
case nearly full, now."

"Oh, what a good idea! Well, I wish you'd
put in that photograph album, and my set of
coral jewelry, and my eye-glasses; and please get
the box of old letters that's on the highest shelf
in that cupboard. Oh, and here's Uncle Ted's
bank-book, we must save that."

"Now, Grace," said Uncle Ted, himself, ap-
pearing in the doorway, "the fire is pretty well
under control; that Harris is a good fellow, and
no mistake. But as the flames may break out
again, I mean to put you out of harm's way at
once. Come out on the balcony."

Uncle Ted had a great coil of rope in his

arms, and he stepped through the long French window onto the balcony, and Aunt Grace and Patty followed. There they discovered quite a party already assembled, and such costumes as they wore !

Mrs. Carleton had on Turkish bedroom slippers, and she wore a black veil tied over her face for fear of smoke. She had wrapped herself in a large eider-down quilt and somebody had tied it round with a wide sash, so that she looked like a queer foreign personage of some sort.

Nan, in her hurry, had fastened her wig on insecurely, and had since lost it. Her attire was an old ulster of Uncle Ted's, which she had found in the third story hall when she ran up to alarm the Carleton children and their nurse.

The nurse in great fright had pulled down portières, and wrapped them round herself and the children, while old Hopalong had shuffled down from her room in a mackintosh and sunbonnet.

To this motley crowd came Aunt Grace in her handsome party gown, and Patty with her bag of treasures.

" Hello, there," cried Uncle Ted, cheerily,

" the danger is over, I think, but we have no stairs left to descend upon. The boys are bringing ladders, however, and I think, with care, we can all get down safely. But as my wife's sprained ankle is scarcely sound enough as yet to trust her on a ladder, I am going to try to swing her down in this hammock. Patty, I think I'll send you down first, for practice."

" All right, Uncle Ted," said Patty, and still clasping her bag of valuables, and wearing Miss Todd's Paris hat, she seated herself in the hammock, exactly according to Uncle Ted's directions, and he and Mr. Carleton carefully let her down by the long ropes which had been fastened at each end of the novel elevator.

Mr. Harris was waiting for her, and he landed her safely on the steps of the lower veranda.

Next Aunt Grace was lowered, and after that another hammock was rigged, and all of the ladies were taken down that way, as they preferred it to the ladders.

The men came down the ladders and brought the little children in their arms, and then the queer-looking crowd gathered in the sitting-room

to discuss the situation. The men concluded
that the fire was occasioned by a mouse having
nibbled at some matches which were kept in the
closet under the stairs.

As the shelves and walls and most of the con-
tents of the closet were charred, it was assumed
that the fire had been smouldering for some
hours, and if Mr. Harris had not discovered it as
soon as he did, it would doubtless have been followed by more disastrous consequences.

The stairs from the first to the second floor
were entirely burned away, and except that the
walls and carpets of both halls were smoked and
discolored, no other harm was done.

But as that staircase was the only one con-
necting the first and second floors, the victims
of the fire found themselves in the peculiar position of not being able to go up-stairs.

" How perfectly ridiculous," exclaimed Aunt
Grace, " to build a house with no back stairs.    I
always said that was the greatest flaw about this
house.   What *can* we do? "

" As it is nearly five o'clock," said Uncle Ted,
" I propose that we have breakfast, and consider
that the day has begun.   Then perhaps I can

get somebody to build stairs or steps of some kind by night."

"But we must go up-stairs," said Nan, who had covered her wigless head with a bandanna kerchief, bound round like a turban; "we want to dress properly before we breakfast."

"And we want to finish our sleep," said Gertrude Carleton. "I'm not going to get up at five o'clock and stay up."

So the ladders were brought in from outside and put up in the stair-well, and with some difficulty everybody was brought safely up-stairs again.

With the procrastination which was characteristic of the Barlow household, the new stairs failed to get built that day or the next either; indeed it was nearly a week before a staircase was put in place, and as it was meant to be only temporary it was made of plain unpainted wood.

But you will not be surprised to learn that it was not replaced by a more sightly affair until after the Barlows had returned to their city home.

As the end of her visit at the Hurly-Burly drew near, Patty felt great regret at the thought of leaving the merry, careless crowd. She invited them, one and all, to visit her when she should be established in her own home, and she promised to correspond regularly with both Bumble and Nan.

"Where is it you're going?" said Bumble, "I never can remember."

"To Vernondale," answered Patty, "a town in New Jersey. But it's nowhere near Elmbridge, where I visited the St. Clairs. I believe it is on another railroad. I've had a lovely letter from Aunt Alice Elliott, and she wants me to come the first week in September. She says Uncle Charlie will meet me in New York, or come over here after me, whichever I say. But I think I'd better meet him in New York."

So when the day came Uncle Ted took Patty over to New York, and Bob and Bumble and Nan went too, and it was a group of very long-faced young people who met Mr. Elliott at the appointed time and place. But Bob said:

"Brace up, girls, we're not losing our Patty forever. She'll spend next summer with us at the Hurly-Burly, and by that time we'll have beautiful new fire-proof stairs."

"Yes," said Bumble, "and she can visit us in Philadelphia in the winter too."

Then after many fond good-byes, the Barlows went away, and Patty was left with her Uncle Charlie.

# CHAPTER XVIII

## AT VERNONDALE

AFTER the Barlows had left them Mr. Elliott put Patty in a cab to go across New York to the New Jersey ferry, and seating himself beside her he said:

"Well, my little maid, I am very glad to get you at last; and as there is a whole houseful of people out at Vernondale who are eagerly watching for your arrival, I am going to get you there as soon as possible."

"Yes, do," said Patty; "I am so anxious to see Marian and all the rest. Tell me something about them, Uncle Charlie. I am getting accustomed to meeting new relatives, but I like to hear about them beforehand, too."

"Well," said Uncle Charlie, "to begin with, your Aunt Alice is the loveliest woman on the face of the earth."

"I am sure she is," said Patty, heartily, "for she has written me such beautiful letters about my coming, and I feel as if I already know her. And then, of course, she is papa's sister, so she must be nice."

"Then there is Grandma Elliott," her uncle went on; "she is my mother, and a dearer old lady never breathed. You'll love her at first sight."

"Oh, I know I shall," said Patty; "there hasn't been a single grandmother in all my other visits, and as I have none of my own, I shall just adopt yours, if she'll let me."

"Try it, and see," said her uncle, smiling. "As to your cousins, they are four specimens of young America who must be seen to be appreciated. Frank is seventeen and Marian is about your own age. Edith is ten, and little Gilbert is six. They are all moderately good and moderately pretty, but on the whole, I think you'll like them."

The travelers crossed the ferry to New Jersey, and after riding nearly an hour in the cars they reached Vernondale.

Mr. Elliott's carriage met them at the railway station, and a short drive brought Patty to her new home. The house was a large one, surrounded by beautiful grounds with fine trees, carefully kept lawns and beds of bright flowers.

The whole family had assembled on the veranda to greet Patty, and as the carriage came up the driveway there was a great waving of handkerchiefs and clapping of hands and shouts of " Here she comes," " Here's our cousin!"

As Uncle Charlie helped Patty out of the carriage, Aunt Alice was the first to clasp her in her arms, and it was with such a warm loving embrace that Patty felt the motherliness of it, and loved her Aunt Alice at once.

Next she was introduced to Grandma Elliott and the dear old lady beamed through her spectacles at pretty Patty, and willingly agreed to adopt her as a really, truly granddaughter.

Cousin Frank proved to be a big, stalwart lad, with merry eyes and a boyish smile, and he welcomed Patty with hearty good-will.

Marian was a beautiful girl with fun and intelligence written all over her bright face, and when she said, " Oh, Patty, I'm *so* glad you've come," Patty felt sure they would be not only warm friends but congenial chums. Ten-year old Edith clasped Patty's hand in both her own and floor, Patty could not repress an exclamation of delight.

"Oh, Aunt Alice," she said, "what a lovely room! Is this mine?"

"Yes, dear," said her aunt, "and I'm glad you like it. It was a great pleasure for Marian and me to arrange it for you."

The room was a large one, with windows on two sides, and the coloring was all pale green and ivory.

The walls were a beautiful shade of light green, with a few water-colors and etchings in narrow gilt or ivory frames.

The carpet was plain green, soft and velvety, like moss; and the furniture, of a light cream-colored wood, was in dainty shapes, with delicate spindle-legged tables and chairs. The dressing-table was furnished with ivory-backed brushes and mirrors, and there was a charming little work-table with sewing materials of all kinds.

An open desk showed every kind of writing-implement, made of ivory or cut-glass, and the blotting-pad was pale green.

A couch by a corner window was provided with many ruffly fluffy pillows, covered with held it for a long while, looking up in her cousin's face with an occasional smile of happy confidence.

Last came little Gilbert, the pet of the household, and a lovely boy he was. Short dark curls clustered all over his head and his great brown eyes gazed at Patty in rapt contemplation.

" I'm glad you've come," he said, finally, " and I love you, and I'll try to be good all the time you're here."

" That's right, my boy," said Uncle Charlie, catching Gilbert up in his arms and setting him on his shoulder, " and after Patty is gone, what then ? "

" Then,—I'll see about it," said the child, gravely, and they all laughed at the carefully considered decision.

Then Aunt Alice took Patty up to her room, and as they went through the halls, Patty thought she had never seen such a beautiful house in her life. It was as large as the St. Clairs' house, but the decorations and furnishings were in subdued tints and quiet effects and there was no loud or garish ornamentation.

When they entered a room on the second

green silk, and a knitted afghan of soft green
wool lay folded at the foot.

Two or three vases of mignonette and ferns
harmonized with the general effect, and gave the
room a delightful fragrance.

Although unable to appreciate all these details
at a first glance, Patty at once realized that the
whole room presented a far more charming and
refined appearance than her more elaborate
apartment at Villa Rosa, with its ornate bric-a-
brac and expensive rugs.

" It is lovely," she said to her aunt.  " I never
saw a room that I liked as well.  I think a fairy
must have touched it with her wand, it is all so
fresh and sweet, just like a woodland dell."

" This is your fairy bower," said Aunt Alice,
and she opened a glass door leading out on a
balcony.

The balcony was as large as a small room, and
it had a roof to it, and rattan shades at the sides
that could be rolled up or down at pleasure.

Vines clambered around the pillars, and on the
railings between them, were palms and bright
flowers growing in jars or tiled boxes.

On the balcony were several easy chairs, a

round table and a couch, all of wicker basket-work, and across the corner was swung a green and white hammock with pillows of green linen.

" Oh, Aunt Alice," cried Patty, " this *is* fairy-land ! Is this *my* balcony ? "

" Yes, dear," said her aunt, kissing her happy, surprised little face, " and I hope you will often enjoy it. I want you to be a happy Patty during your stay with us."

" I am happy already," said Patty, as they went back into her room, " in such a lovely home, and among such lovely people."

" May I come in ? " said Marian, tapping at the open door. " Mother mine, are you going to monopolize our Patty ? I haven't half seen her yet."

" You can see me," said Patty, smiling at her cousin, " but you can't hear me, for I am speechless with delight at this beautiful room, and that fairy-land place outside. And now I'm going to put my mother's picture on the desk and then it will be just perfect."

Patty took the portrait from her traveling-bag, and Aunt Alice looked at it tenderly. Though she had known her brother's young wife but a short time, she had greatly loved and admired her.

"You are like your mother, Patty," she said.

"So every one tells me, Aunt Alice. But I want to be a Fairfield too. Don't you think I am like papa?"

"Not very much in appearance. Perhaps you are like him in disposition. I'll wait until I know you better before I judge. Brother Fred was the stubbornest boy I ever saw. But when I told him so, he said it was only firmness of character."

"I think that's what it is with papa," said Patty, loyally, "but I've often heard him say that I used to be very stubborn when I was little."

"It's a Fairfield trait," said Aunt Alice, smiling, and as Patty looked at the sweet-faced lady she thought she seemed as if perhaps she could be very firm if occasion required.

"Marian," said Patty, "Aunt Alice says you helped arrange this lovely room for me, and I want to thank you and tell you how much I admire it."

"Oh, I didn't do much," said Marian. "I only selected the books and stocked the writing-desk

and  sewing-table, and made the sofa-pillows and
did a few little things like that.  Mamma did most
of it  herself.  And grandma knitted the afghan.
Isn't it pretty?  We were all glad to get ready
for your coming.  We've looked forward to it
ever since you came North."

"Come, Marian," said her mother, "let us run
away now, and leave Patty to dress for dinner.
Unless we can help you unpack, may we?  Your
trunks have come, and I will have them sent up
here at once."

"Oh, yes, let me help you put away your
things," said Marian, but Patty, with a slight
blush, thanked them for their kind offers but declined their assistance.  And for a very good
reason, or at least it seemed so to the embarrassed child.  During her stay at the Hurly-
Burly, poor Patty's wardrobe had become sadly
dilapidated.

It never occurred to the Barlow family to
mend their clothes.  Missing buttons were never
replaced except by pins; torn ends of trimming
were left hanging or snipped off; and after a
whole summer's carelessness, Patty's garments
were in a deplorable state.

So the child really felt ashamed for her aunt and cousin, who seemed to be the quintessence of neatness, to discover her untidy wardrobe.

Even her best dresses were soiled and wrinkled. Nan and Bumble had helped her to pack, and their idea of packing a trunk seemed to be to toss everything in in a heap, and then jump on the lid to make it shut tight.

So woful Patty looked over her clothes in dismay. They had seemed all right down at the Hurly-Burly, but here, in this immaculate green and white room they seemed utterly out of place, and quite unworthy of being put away in the bureau-drawers or cupboards.

It was with difficulty that she decided upon a dress to wear down to dinner. Her light summer dresses had been bought ready-made during one of Aunt Grace's hurried trips to New York, and with the well-known viciousness of ready-made clothing, had shrunk and stretched in the wrong places, and showed occasional rips besides. Then being badly laundered and afterwards crumpled in the trunk, they presented anything but the fresh, crisp appearance that summer dresses ought to have.

So Patty looked over her other frocks. But the gorgeous ones that she hadn't worn since she was at Aunt Isabel's, seemed more than ever in glaring bad taste, and as she had needed no new clothes at Aunt Hester's, she had bought none while in Boston.

With a sigh, she selected a pink muslin, that did fairly well, except that the lace was gone from one sleeve and two buttons were missing.

She ripped the lace from the other sleeve, so that they might match, at least, and was rejoiced to find that there were some buttons in a drawer of her new work-table.

Of course needles and thread were there too, which was fortunate, for Patty had none in her trunk, and indeed, she scarcely knew how to use them anyway.

As she dressed, she resolved that she would confide her troubles to Aunt Alice, and ask help in replenishing her wardrobe.

" I'm all out of proportion," she said to herself, " and papa wouldn't like it a bit if he knew that I didn't have a decent dress to put on. But down at the Hurly-Burly nobody cared or thought anything about it."

As all her shoes seemed to lack some buttons or to have broken laces, she put on her best slippers, and after she had brushed her pretty hair, and improved the despised pink muslin with some bows of black velvet, she looked quite presentable, and if Aunt Alice noticed anything amiss she gave no hint of it to her young guest.

# CHAPTER XIX

## A PICNIC

" Aunt Alice," said Patty, the next morning after breakfast, " I want to have a little talk with you, and won't you come up to my Fairy Bower so we can be by ourselves,—for it's a sort of secret ? "

" I will, my child," said Aunt Alice, " as soon as I've attended to a few household duties. I'll meet you there, in about half an hour. Will your secret keep that long ? "

" Oh, yes indeed ; I'm in no hurry at all."

" I don't seem to be included in the secret," said Marian ; " but come with me, Patty, won't you, until mamma is ready for you ? I'm going to water the palms and plants in the front veranda. That is always part of my morning's work."

" Let me help you," said Patty, and the two girls went off together.

In a short time Aunt Alice reappeared, saying, "Now, Patty girl, I'm at your disposal. Marian, dear, remember this is Thursday, and the Basket Drill is at ten."

"Yes, I know, mamma. I'll be ready for it."

When Mrs. Elliott was comfortably seated in a rocking-chair on the balcony, Patty drew up a small wicker stool and sat down in front of her.

"Aunt Alice," she began, "my secret is just this. I haven't any clothes that are fit to wear, and I want you to help me get some. When I was at Aunt Isabel's she bought me loads of dresses, but they were all winter ones, and besides, I don't believe they're the kind you'd like. In Boston, at Aunt Hester's, nobody ever thought much about what they wore, and I got along all right, somehow, but this summer down at Aunt Grace's, my clothes seemed to go to pieces all at once."

"Like the 'One-Hoss-Shay,'" said Aunt Alice, laughing. "Well, this is indeed a sad state of affairs. But perhaps we can find a way out of the difficulty."

"Yes, of course we can," said Patty, eagerly. "Papa sends me money whenever I ask him for it; so if you'll buy me some clothes, he'll repay you at once. I want everything. My things are no good at all."

"Wait, wait," said Aunt Alice, "don't dispose of your wardrobe in such a summary way. Suppose we look it over together, and see what's best to be done."

"All right," said Patty, "but I'm really ashamed to show you the miserable lot."

"Why, Patty," said Aunt Alice, as she looked over the torn and crumpled dresses and under-clothing, "these do seem to be unwearable, but they are not hopelessly so. You see, the trouble is, they've been neglected, and clothes, like plants or children, won't thrive under neglect."

"I know it, Aunt Alice, but we never thought of mending things down at the Hurly-Burly, and there was no one to do it for us, as there was at Aunt Isabel's."

"Never mind your other aunts, Patty; you have to deal now with your Aunt Alice, and you will find her a regular tyrant."

But the loving smile which accompanied this speech robbed it of all tyrannical effect.

"Now," the "tyrant" went on, "we'll put in one pile all the things that are too faded or worn to be of use to you, and those we'll give away to some one who can use them. These heavy silk and velvet frocks and these gorgeous party dresses we'll just lay away for the present, and now we'll put in this place all that needs mending. It's a shame to see these dainty little white petticoats and nightgowns with their buttons off, and their trimmings torn."

" Yes, Aunt Isabel bought me those, and they were lovely when they were new."

" And they'll be lovely again, for they only need a few stitches and some good laundry-work to make them as pretty and fresh as ever. Do you know how to sew, Patty ? "

"No, Aunt Alice, I don't. When I was at home, Mrs. Miller, our landlady, always looked after my things, and I never thought of sewing ; and since I've been North, I haven't, either."

" Well, Patty, sewing is an old-fashioned accomplishment, I suppose, but I think it is something that every woman ought to know ; and if you are going to keep my brother's house for him, I am going to see to it that you are well equipped for the task, and to that end I'm going to instruct you in both sewing and housekeeping. There, Miss Patty Fairfield, how do you like that ? "

Patty ran to her aunt's arms, which were open to receive her, and kissed her lovingly.

" Oh, Aunt Alice, I'll be so glad if you will, for I do want to keep papa's house right. But Aunt Grace told me not to worry about it, and the house would keep itself."

" Never mind Aunt Grace now, you are under Aunt Alice's orders, as I told you. And she was right in telling you not to worry about it; but as to a house keeping itself, I haven't heard that the autohome has been invented yet, and until it is, we'll stand by the old methods of housekeeping. And so, every morning, my dear Patty, unless something very important calls you elsewhere, you are to spend two hours with me, in studying what the wise people call Domestic Science, but I call Domestic Common-sense."

Patty's little face looked very bright and happy, for she was truly anxious to learn these things, and there had been no opportunities during her other visits.

" I treat Marion in the same way," said Aunt

Alice. "Although we have several servants,
Marian has learned and practiced many branches
of housework and she sews very nicely. But I
don't think you will find Marian 'worried' or
even impatient at the irksome tasks."

"No, indeed, Aunt Alice, Marian is as bright
and cheery as a sunbeam, and I'm sure no task
could be irksome if you advised or assisted with it."

"Oh, you don't know me yet," laughed Aunt
Alice; "didn't I tell you I was a tyrant? But
you do need some new things, child, and we'll
buy them in a day or two."

Aunt Alice counted over the dresses which
could be make available for use, and then, select-
ing a number of garments only slightly out of
repair, she said:

"This morning we'll attack these. Did you
hear me tell Marian to remember the Basket
Drill? Well, that means the sewing or mending basket; and if you'll bring yours with you,
we'll attend a Ladies' Sewing Society in the sitting-room at once."

In the sitting-room they found Marian with
her basket of work, and grandma, who was
darning stockings.

With kindly care and patience Aunt Alice showed Patty how to mend neatly, and as the pupil was by no means stupid, she did great credit to her teacher.

After they had sewed for about an hour, Mrs. Elliott said:

" Now, children, put away your baskets and run out to play. You need fresh air and sunshine quite as much as buttons and strings. Marian, why don't you take Patty down and show her the Falls? You'll have just about time enough to go and get back to luncheon."

" We will," said Marian; " come along, Patty."

As Patty was by nature adaptable to her surroundings, she followed Marian's example and arranged her work-basket tidily and then put it away in its place, though down at the Hurly-Burly it would never have occurred to her to do so, and nobody would have set her such an example.

Patty thought to herself, " Well, these people have the right proportion of system and order, anyhow; I wonder if they're lacking in some other proportion. I haven't seen it yet, if they are."

And she didn't discover it later, either; for though not perfect people, by any means, the Elliotts had a true sense of proportion, and no duty or pleasure was pursued to excess, and so allowed to crowd out other duties or pleasures.

" Mother," said Frank, as they sat on the veranda, one evening, soon after Patty's arrival, " I think we might have a picnic in Patty's honor. I want her to get acquainted with the boys and girls, and that's as good a way as any. And if we could have it on Saturday afternoon, perhaps father could take a half-holiday and go with us."

" That's a fine idea," said Aunt Alice; " do you agree, Charlie?"

" Yes," said Mr. Elliott, " I'd like it of all things. Shall we go to Foster's Woods?"

" Yes," said Marian, " that's the nicest place for a picnic. There's a lovely lake there, Patty, and boats to row about in, and tables for the feast and everything."

" How many shall you invite?" said Uncle Charlie. " I'll engage stages to take us all over."

" I want to go," said Edith. " Mayn't I, mamma?"

" Of course you may," said Mrs. Elliott; " we'll

take the whole family, from grandma down to little Gilbert."

" Oh, I can't go," said grandma; " I'm too old for picnics."

" Not a bit," said her son; " if you don't care for staging, I'll send you and Alice and the baby over in the carriage."

And then they all fell to planning the details of the picnic, and Patty secretly contrasted the occasion with similar ones at her other aunts'.

There was no quarreling about arrangements as at Villa Rosa; each deferred politely to the others' opinions, and yet each frankly expressed his or her mind on any subject.

And there was no inattention or forgetfulness as at the Hurly-Burly. Each was appointed to attend to several different things, and Patty felt sure that their promises would all be fulfilled.

" Let's have lots of sandwiches," said Frank; " the last picnic I went to, I didn't have half enough. And can't we have jam in some of them, as well as chicken and ham ?"

" Certainly, my boy," said his mother; " I'll see that you have jam sandwiches and ham sandwiches and chicken sandwiches, and plenty of them."

"Those names might be shortened," said Uncle Charlie, meditatively. "The *sand* is superfluous, anyway. There's no sand in them. Why don't we say jamwiches, hamwiches and chickwiches?"

"Oh, that's much better," cried Marian. "I wonder we never thought of it before. I shall never mention a ham sandwich again. A hamwich is so much nicer."

"And then there are tonguewiches and eggwiches," said Patty, delighted with the new words.

"And jellywiches," said Aunt Alice, laughing. "And now what else do young people eat? Cakes and fruit, I suppose."

"Yes, and little tarts," said Frank; "they're awfully good on a picnic."

"And ice cream," said Marian.

"I'll order the ice cream," said her father, "and I'll bring a big box of candies from New York. Frank, you must see to the hammocks and swings, and games if you want them."

"Yes, sir," said Frank, "I'll take my shuffleboard and ring-toss. And we'll build a fire, and make coffee, shall we mother?"

" Yes, dear; Patty and I will make the coffee," said Aunt Alice with a sidelong smile at her niece.

" Then I know it will be good," said Frank.

Saturday was a beautiful day, clear and bright and not too warm.

Immediately after luncheon four stages went around and gathered up about fifty young people, and a wagon full of provisions for feasting and fun followed them to Foster's Woods.

Patty wore a pretty white frock, which, under Aunt Alice's instruction, she had neatly mended, and Mrs. Elliott's skilful laundress had made clean and crisp.

The Vernondale young people proved to be a merry, jolly crowd, and pretty Patty soon became a favorite.

Frank and Mariam introduced her to everybody and took special care that she should never lack for companions or amusement.

And there was so much to do, and Patty enjoyed it all. She was clever at the games, and owing to her practice at the Hurly-Burly, she could row as well as any boy.

The lake was a beautiful bit of water, and in some parts of it pond-lilies grew in abundance.

The young people gathered a quantity of these, both white and pink, to decorate the supper-table.

Then when the feast was ready, Uncle Charlie called the children together, and they came with a will, for their afternoon out of doors had given them a good appetite for the hamwiches and jamwiches.

After supper was over, it was about seven o'clock, and Uncle Charlie told his young guests that they could ramble round for half an hour, and then they would start on their homeward ride.

The path by the side of the lake was a very pretty one, and Mrs. Elliott and her husband walked along there with little Gilbert between them. The child was getting sleepy and a little wilful; and while Jane, his nurse, was eating her supper, his parents had him in charge.

Soon they heard Frank's voice calling, " Father, won't you please come here a minute and help us get this swing down? "

Mr. Elliott went to help the boys, and Mrs.

Elliott and Gilbert sat down on the grassy bank to await his return.

" Mamma," said the child, " shall I pick you some pretty flowers ? "

" Yes, baby," said his mother, who was looking at the sunset, and only half listening, " but don't go far away."

" No," said the little fellow, and how it happened, Mrs. Elliott never knew, but seemingly in a moment, Gilbert had climbed into a boat and was afloat alone on the lake. For an instant Mrs. Elliott was too frightened even to scream; and then, she dared not, for the boat was a little, round-bottomed affair, and Gilbert was jumping about in it so excitedly, that if suddenly startled he might upset the boat.

With great presence of mind his mother spoke to him gently.

" Gilbert, dear," she said, " sit down in the middle of the boat, and be quiet until I call papa, will you? There's a good boy."

" I am a good boy," Gilbert called back ; " I'm going to get mamma pretty pink pond-flowers."

The boat was drifting farther and farther out,

and the child sitting in the bow, rocked it from one side to the other.

"Gilbert," said his mother, sternly, "sit right down in the bottom of the boat. Right in the middle, do you hear? Obey me at once!"

"Yes, mamma," said the boy, and he did as she told him to, but continued to rock the boat, so though the danger was lessened, it was still a frightful scene, and filled the poor mother's heart with terror.

"Charlie, Charlie," she called, and then "Frank," but they could not hear her as they were taking down some hammocks in another part of the grove.

The boat drifted nearer to the pond-lilies, and Mrs. Elliott saw Gilbert lean over the side of the boat.

"Now I'll get them for you, mamma," he called.

Mrs. Elliott could sarcely hear his words, but she saw,—the boat overturn and her darling child fall into the deep lake.

# CHAPTER XX

## THE RESCUE

WHEN Mrs. Elliott called to her husband and son, they could not hear her, but her cries were heard by a small group of half-a-dozen boys and girls, who were walking along the shore of the lake at some distance ahead of her.

Patty and Marian were in this group, and at the sound of her mother's frightened cry, Marian turned pale, and said, "Oh, Patty, something dreadful has happened; let us run to mother."

But one of the boys said, "Look out on the lake! There's your little brother in a boat, all alone."

"Oh," cried Marian, "he'll be upset! Where's papa? Can any of you boys swim?"

"No," said two of the boys, and another said, "I can't either, but I'm going to try."

"Don't do it," said Patty, who was already flinging off her shoes. "I can swim, and I'll save the baby."

She remembered how Nan jumped into the water with her ordinary clothes on that day at the Hurly-Burly, and so she ran into the lake, all dressed as she was, for there was no time to lose, and struck out for the boat.

She had taken but a few strokes, when she saw the child fall into the water, and heard Mrs. Elliott give a despairing shriek.

Patty gave one shout of "All right, Aunt Alice, I'll get him!" and then swam for dear life. This was literally true, for she was determined to save the dear life of little Gilbert if she possibly could.

And she did, for as the baby rose to the surface, Patty was near enough to grasp him, and then managed to reach the overturned boat and by its support she easily kept herself and the child afloat.

"He's all right," she called to the crowd now gathering on the bank. "I can hold him up; somebody come out after us in a boat." But two boats had already started, and in a few minutes Gilbert was lifted into one and Patty scrambled into the other, and they were quickly rowed ashore, and when they landed on the beach,

Uncle Charlie, with the tears rolling down his cheeks, tried to embrace both Patty and Gilbert at once.

Aunt Alice couldn't speak, but the looks of love and gratitude she gave Patty said more than words could, and Patty felt that this was the happiest moment of her life. And what a fuss the young people made over her! The boys praised her pluck, and the girls marveled at her skill.

But as Patty and Gilbert were both dripping wet, and it was already nightfall, the question was, what to do to keep them from taking cold.

" Build up the fire again," said grandma, " and we'll undress the baby, and wrap him all up in one of the carriage robes."

" And there's another carriage robe for Patty," said Marian.

" I'll fix Patty," said Uncle Charlie, " haven't some of you girls a big blanket-shawl that won't be spoiled if it gets wet? "

Several shawls were eagerly offered, and Uncle Charlie selected two big warm ones and wrapped Patty, wet clothes and all, tightly in them, leaving only her face exposed, until she looked like a mummy, and was wound so tight she couldn't stand up without assistance. But Uncle Charlie took the laughing mummy in his arms and lifted her right into his carriage and then got in and sat beside her.

"Now give me the baby," he said, and Gilbert, equally wrapped up, was put into his arms.

"Help your mother and grandma in, Frank," he said, "and then, my son, you must look after your guests, and see that the stages are filled and started off. We will drive home quickly and I think our Patty and Gilbert will suffer no harm from their bath. You and Marian must explain all this, and say good-bye to our guests. It has been a terrible experience, but we are all safe now, and I don't want the young people to feel saddened."

"Yes, father," said Frank, "I'll take charge here, and look after Marian and Edith, and attend to getting everything and everybody home safely."

Then the driver took up his whip, and Mr. Elliott's horses flew over the ground at a mad pace.

Although the sudden fright had shocked Mrs. Elliott terribly, she was beginning to recover herself, and by the time the carriage reached home, she was all ready to take charge of affairs in her usual capable way. Uncle Charlie deposited the bundle of baby on the sofa, and then went back and carried in what he called his " mummy niece."

" Grandma," said Mrs. Elliott, " I'll give our darling Patty into your charge, for the present. Will you see that she has a hot bath, and a steaming hot drink made after one of your good old recipes ? And then tuck her into her bed in double-quick time. After I treat baby in a similar fashion, and get him to sleep, I will interview my niece myself."

And when that interview took place, Patty was made to know how deep a mother's gratitude can be, and the bond sealed that night between Aunt Alice and her niece was one of lifelong endurance and deep, true love.

Next day, the Water Babies, as Uncle Charlie called Patty and Gilbert, were as well as ever, and suffered no ill effects from their dip in the lake.

Many of the Vernondale boys and girls came to see Patty, and Frank and Marian exhibited her with pride, as if she were an Imperial treasure

Patty bore her honors modestly, for it didn't seem to her that she had done anything specially meritorious. She was glad Bob and Uncle Ted had taught her to swim so well, and even greater than her joy at saving Gilbert's life was the thought that she had saved the boy for her dear Aunt Alice whom she loved so much

When Uncle Charlie came home from New York that night, he brought Patty a beautiful gold brooch set with pearls and with a sparkling diamond in the centre.

" This isn't a reward, Patty dear," he said, " for no amount of jewels could represent the value of our baby's life. But I want you to wear it sometimes as heroes wear the Victoria Cross, or as men at the life-saving stations wear their medals."

Patty's heart was touched at this expression of Uncle Charlie's gratitude, and she was delighted, too, with the beautiful gift.

" I don't want any reward, uncle," she said, " but I shall keep this lovely brooch all my life as one of my choicest treasures."

# CHAPTER XXI

## A READING-CLUB

WITH October came school-days.

There was a fine school for young ladies in Vernondale, which Marian attended, and Aunt Alice thought it best for Patty to go too.

The cousins, who had become inseparable companions, enjoyed their school-life together, and the added duties which lessons brought, caused Aunt Alice to make Patty's household tasks rather fewer.

That lady was by no means an advocate of "all work and no play," and though some domestic duties were imposed and a cake or a dessert was taught every Saturday, yet Patty had plenty of time for amusements and plenty of amusements for her time.

One October day, Patty and Marian and two of their schoolgirl friends sat on Patty's balcony drinking afternoon tea.

It was getting late in the season to use the

pretty balcony, but it chanced to be a bright, sunny autumn day, and the girls had their wraps on.

Besides, they were talking so busily, that I think they would scarcely have noticed it, had the mercury suddenly fallen to zero.

"Yes," Elsie Morris was saying, "we'll have a real literary club, and we'll have a president and constitution and everything. But don't let's have too many members. About twelve girls, I should say."

"Only girls?" said Marian, "aren't we going to have any boys? I know Frank would like to join."

"Oh, boys don't like to read," said Polly Stevens, "they're nice at parties and picnics, but we want this club to be really literary, and not just fooling."

"I know it," said Marian, "but we thought we'd have little plays and tableaux, and things like that. And how can we manage those without boys? What do you say, Patty?"

"I think it's nice to have the boys," said Patty, "but they won't come much in the afternoons. If we have them, it'll have to be an evening affair. Let's ask Aunt Alice."

" Yes," said Elsie, " Mrs. Elliott always knows just what to do."

" I'll go after her," said Patty, and away she ran, and returned in triumph with her aunt.

" Now, my blessed auntie," she said, as she gave her a seat, and wrapped a fleecy shawl about her shoulders, " let me offer you a cup of tea, for we are going to give you a weighty question to decide, and you'll need a stimulant."

" Very well," said Aunt Alice, laughing, " but you'd better ask the question quickly, for this tea doesn't look very strong and its effects will soon wear off."

So the girls all talked at once, or at least, two at a time, and explained that they wanted a literary club, and while they all liked the boys and would be glad of their assistance in plays and tableaux, yet they knew that if boys came to the meetings, there'd be little or no serious reading done.

" It may be the effects of your tea," said Mrs. Elliott, " but the solution of your problem seems to me so easy that I wonder you didn't think it out for yourselves."

" Oh, what is it?" said Elsie and Marian together.

" Why, have your club of girls only, and have your meetings on Saturday afternoons, as you proposed, and then occasionally,—say, once a month,—have an evening meeting and invite the boys and have your dramatic or musical entertainments then."

" I knew you'd fix it, Aunt Alice," said Patty, beaming, " won't that be just right, girls ? "

They all agreed to this wise plan, and immediately made out a list of twelve girls, who, if they accepted the invitation, were to attend the first club meeting at Elsie Morris's house on the following Saturday.

Every one did accept, and the club was formed, and the twelve members went to work with a will to make rules and plans.

Patty was unanimously elected president.

She hesitated about undertaking to fill such a responsible office, but the girls, one and all, insisted upon it in a determined if not very parliamentary way ; and so she accepted the position, feeling sure that Aunt Alice would assist and advise her in any difficulties that might arise.

The Literary Club proved a great success. Patty made a very capable and graceful little president, and when at a meeting in November, the girls began to discuss an evening entertainment to be held in December, and Patty remarked that perhaps she wouldn't be in Vernondale then, a general outcry was raised.

"What do you mean?"

"Why not?"

"Why, Patty Fairfield, where are you going?"

"I don't know where I'm going," said Patty, "but my visit at Marian's will be over the first of December, and then I'm going to have a new home, and I don't know where it will be. But oh, girls, I wish it could be in Vernondale."

"Why can't it?" said Marian eagerly, "why can't Uncle Fred buy a house here, and then you can live here all your life. Oh, Patty, wouldn't that be just fine?"

"Oh, Patty, do!" chorused all the girls, and Patty resolved that if she had any voice in the matter, Vernondale should be her future home.

## CHAPTER XXII

### A WELCOME GUEST

"Oh, Aunt Alice," cried Patty, flying into her aunt's room one morning in the latter part of November, "I've just had a letter from papa, and he'll be here for Thanksgiving-day! Isn't that grand?" and catching her aunt round the waist, Patty waltzed her up and down the room until the good lady was nearly breathless.

"I'm as glad as you are, Patty girl," she said, when her niece finally allowed her to come to a standstill, "for I haven't seen brother Fred for many long years. But I can tell you that his coming doesn't by any means bring your visit to an end; I'm going to keep you both here with me until after the holidays, and longer too, if I can."

"Well, I'll be only too glad to stay as long as papa is willing, and I do hope I can persuade him to settle in Vernondale. *Do* you believe he will, Aunt Alice?"

"I don't know. I think he is inclined to make his home in New York city. But Vernondale is a pleasant place and so near New York, as to be a sort of suburb."

"Well, I'm going to coax him, anyhow,—and now Aunt Alice, I'm going to ask you a big, big favor, may I?"

"Yes, you may ask, but I won't make any rash promises to grant it, until I hear what it is."

"Well,—I'm afraid you'll think I won't make them good enough,—but—I do want to make the pumpkin pies for Thanksgiving-day. Papa would be so surprised and pleased."

"Why, of course you may, child; I'll be very glad to be relieved of that duty, and cook will have all she can attend to."

"When is Uncle Fred coming?" said Frank, as they all sat at dinner that evening.

"The night before Thanksgiving," said Patty; "he'll arrive at about nine o'clock."

"Well, we'll give him a rousing welcome," said Frank, "a sort of 'Harvest Home,' you know."

"All right," said his father, who was ever ready for a frolic, "what can we do out of the ordinary?"

" We could decorate the veranda with jack-o'-lanterns," said Marian, " and he'll see them as he drives up."

" Just the thing," said Frank, " and, oh,—I have a fine plan, but we won't tell Patty,—at least, not yet."

The day before Thanksgiving, the children were all allowed to stay home from school to make the final preparations for Uncle Fred's reception.

While Patty was in the kitchen making her pumpkin pies, (and surely, such beautiful pies never were made, before or since!) there was much rushing in and out of the parlor; and sounds of hammering and of moving furniture reached Patty's ears, but she was told that she would not be allowed even to peep into the room until evening.

So after the pies were made, Patty ran up to put the finishing touches to her father's bed-room.

She filled the vases with fresh flowers, laid out a new book which she had bought as a welcom-ing gift for him, and on his dressing-table she placed the cherished portrait of her mother; and talking to the picture as she often did, she said :

" I'm going to lend you to him, motherdy, for a few days; I shall miss you, of course, but we want to give him the very best welcome possible."

Patty was allowed to help with all the preparations except those in the parlor, and she was extremely curious to know what was going on in there. But she found plenty to occupy her time, for the whole house was to be decorated.

On the veranda railing were many "jack-o'-lanterns," which when their candles were lighted would flash a welcome from their wide, funny mouths and round eyes.

The hall was decorated with boughs of evergreen, among which were tiny yellow squashes and gourds, also cut like jack-o'-lanterns and holding small candles.

The sitting-room was decorated with bunches of grain, and red peppers, " for," said Frank, " it won't be a Harvest Home, unless we have grain and winter vegetables."

After all was ready, Patty went to don the pretty dress which Aunt Alice and she had bought for the great occasion.

It was a dainty little blue and white striped silk, with ruffles edged with narrow black velvet. The yoke and sleeves were of fine white embroidered muslin, and very fair and sweet Patty looked as she clasped her " Victoria Cross " at her throat.

" Now can I go in the parlor, Frank ? " she said, as she met her cousin on the stairs.

" Yes, Patsy, come along," and the boy threw open the parlor doors with a flourish. The room was elaborately trimmed with palms and chrysanthemums, and at one end was a raised platform, like a throne, on which stood a large armchair draped with a red velvet portière. Above this was a semicircular canopy cleverly made of cornstalks and bunches of grain and up on the very top was the biggest pumpkin you ever saw cut like a jack-o'-lantern.

More tall cornstalks formed a background to the throne and at each side stood a noble sheaf of wheat. Thickly scattered over the whole affair were gourds or mock-oranges, which had been hollowed out and held lighted tapers, while across the top was " welcome " in large letters made of gilt paper.

"Oh," said Patty, quite awestruck at this bright and novel scene, "what is it all for?"

"Tell her, mother," said Frank to Aunt Alice, who had just come in, "I must go and listen for the carriage."

"It's for you, Patty," said her aunt; "you are to sit there and welcome your father when he comes, and you'd better jump into the chair now, for he may be here at any minute."

"Oh, how kind you all are," said Patty. "Did Frank do all this for me? Won't papa be pleased?"

Patty flew up the steps and settled herself in the great chair with delight.

"That's all right," said Marian, who had just come in and who gave a critical glance at the whole picture. "Now *stay* there, Patty; don't jump down when you hear us greet Uncle Fred in the hall."

"I won't," said Patty, "I'll stay," and in another minute the carriage drove up, and Patty heard her father's voice greeting Aunt Alice and her cousins, and then saying, "But where's Patty? Where's my girl?"

"Here, papa," cried Patty, mindful of her

promise to sit still, but unable to resist calling to him, and then Mr. Fairfield hurried into the parlor and saw his pretty daughter enthroned to welcome him.

But at sight of his dear face, Patty *couldn't* sit still, and she flew out of her chair and was in her father's arms before he was half-way across the room.

Nobody minded, however, for there was such a chattering and laughing and frolicking as you never saw, and all the time Mr. Fairfield kept his arm around his little daughter as if he would never let her leave him again.

" But don't think your beautiful work isn't appreciated, my boy," he said to Frank, as Patty called his attention to the cleverly constructed throne, " indeed, I think now is the time to put it to use," and Mr. Fairfield seated himself in the big chair and drew Patty down upon his knee.

Then Frank led off in three hearty cheers for Uncle Fred and Patty, and the Elliott family joined in with a will.

And what a merry, happy Thanksgiving-day they had on the morrow !

Patty's pies were praised until the little maid blushed at the compliments she received.

It was late in the afternoon before father and daughter found an opportunity for a little talk by themselves; and then Patty told of her love and admiration for Aunt Alice, and her great desire to spend the rest of her life in Vernondale.

"For you see, papa," she said, "Aunt Alice is the only one of my aunts who has a sense of proportion, and she certainly has. She is rich, but she doesn't talk about it like Aunt Isabel's people; she reads, and knows a lot about books, but she doesn't seem to think there's nothing else in the world *but* books, as Aunt Hester's family does; and as for the Hurly-Burly people, they're lovely in some ways,—but, after living with Aunt Alice, I couldn't stand their forgetfulness and carelessness. And then, Aunt Alice has everything in her life, and not too much of anything either. We children have lots of fun and good times, but we have to work some, too. And Aunt Alice teaches us to be kind and polite without making any fuss about it. And she does beautiful charity work, and she's so happy and sweet that everybody loves her. And papa,